Between Heaven and Hell

Sherryl D. Hancock

Published by Vulpine Press in the United Kingdom in 2019

ISBN: 978-1-83919-292-0

Cover by Claire Wood

Cover photo credit: Tirzah D. Hancock

www.vulpine-press.com

Also in the *WeHo* series:

Prologue

"Just put your hands where I can see them!"

Catalina was in a San Diego bar called Gossip Grill—more specifically, in the bathroom. She'd seen a blond, butch-looking woman dealing in the club, and as a cop she couldn't allow that. So she'd followed her to the bathroom, waited until everyone was out but her, and moved to arrest her, while Jovina stood guard outside to keep everyone else out.

"If you'll just—" the woman started to say, moving her hand toward her jacket.

"Put your fucking hands up or I'm going to assume you're going for a gun," Catalina growled.

"And if you blow my fucking cover, I'll assume you're dumber than you look," the woman growled right back.

Catalina narrowed her blue eyes. "You said what?" she said, glancing behind her to make sure no one was coming into the bathroom.

"Badge 4578, LAPD—check it out. But in the meantime, can I put my hands down?"

Catalina was shocked. "Yeah. Yeah, sorry. Why are you this far south?"

"Followed a lead." The woman turned around and leaned a hip against the bathroom sink, looking Catalina over with her green eyes.

"You're a cop?" she asked cynically.

"DOJ, Special Agent Supervisor for LA IMPACT," Cat said, even as she texted the information to her CLETS people to ensure that this woman was telling the truth.

"And what are you doing this far south, SAS…"

"Roché," Catalina supplied. "Catalina Roché. And I'm on vacation."

The woman grinned. "I take it your hot Latina is keeping our fellow lesbians at bay?"

Catalina laughed. "Yeah," she said, nodding as her contact came back with information. "So, Sinclair Christensen." She smiled, reaching into her back pocket and pulling out her wallet, then took out a card. "If you ever want to change directions, I supervise the counter-meth team with DOJ. Give me a call."

Sinclair nodded, pocketing the card. "Does everyone in this place know you're a cop?" she asked, with a grin that made her eyes sparkle.

"No one here knows I'm a cop—this is my first time here," Catalina said. "So you're free to join us for a drink if you'd like."

"Done."

They spent the rest of the evening drinking, talking, and having a generally good time. Catalina gave Sinclair the names of her previous team members—all narcs with San Diego PD—in the event she needed some backup while in the city. She also told Sinclair to look them up in LA when she returned—that a group of them hung out at the Club in West Hollywood.

"Not too close to your cover, is it?" Catalina asked. She knew

Sinclair would need to keep a buffer between where she hung out and where she worked.

"Nope, I'm down in Watts."

"Then come hang," Catalina said, smiling.

Sinclair nodded. "I just might."

Two nights later, she crawled into bed next to a hot young redhead.

"You're back," the woman said as she turned over, snuggling into Sinclair's arms.

"Mmhmm," Sinclair murmured, sliding her hands over smooth skin. "Ended up in San Diego."

"Way down there?"

"Yeah," Sinclair said, pulling her closer in an effort to distract her—it worked.

"Mmm... Sin..." the girl sighed, pressing her lips to Sinclair's skin.

Minutes later they were making love, and she didn't ask any more questions.

Later, River lay looking up at Sinclair. She knew she'd purposely distracted her from asking questions. She liked that Sinclair wanted to keep her out of her business. It bothered River that Sinclair was a drug dealer; what also bothered her was what she'd heard about the woman: that she was dangerous and couldn't be trusted. She'd never found that to be true in the entire time she'd known her. Granted, that was only three months so far, but Sinclair had never been anything but kind to her. One man had told her that Sinclair had killed people, shooting them in the head over a drug deal going bad.

River tried not to think about that. She knew being with this woman was probably the craziest thing she'd ever done, but she didn't care. Sinclair was incredibly exciting, and attractive in a sporty, butch kind of way, with long blond hair that was always pulled back, beautiful green eyes, and a long, lean body with just enough muscle to keep her from being skinny. River knew she was addicted to Sinclair. She was the first woman she'd ever been so highly sexually attracted to, and she knew that was part of the problem. Her body couldn't give this woman up, even if her head told her she was crazy.

As a nurse, River McCall had never pictured herself as the girlfriend of a drug dealer. She truly hated drugs, and saw the effects of them every day at the clinic she worked in. It didn't seem to matter when Sinclair pulled her into her arms; she lost all sense of reason.

She fell asleep, her hand on Sinclair's cheek.

A week later, Sinclair entered a house in Bel Air, dropping her keys into the antique Imari plate on the antique foyer table. Walking through the house, she checked through the mail, tossing it on the marble counter in the kitchen. She went to the refrigerator and pulled out a beer, then opened it and tossed the cap on the counter, grinning because she knew it would drive Tracey insane if she left it there.

"All the more reason to do it," she said.

She went into their bedroom. Setting her beer down, she stripped off her "butch gear," as she referred to it most of the time. She stepped into the steam shower and cleaned up, washing her hair. Afterward she put on a pair of yoga pants and an LA Galaxy tank top. Moving out to the veranda overlooking Los Angeles, she drank her beer and read her text messages.

Catalina was inviting her to the Club again. It did sound like it could be an interesting trip to make. Tracey abhorred WeHo—she said it was "too gay." It made Sinclair roll her eyes every time, and it also made her want to remind Tracey that she was technically gay. She hadn't done it, just because she didn't want to get into a big, wicked fight with her, and they always got ugly these days. Just wasn't worth the stress.

Leaning back, turning her face up to the summer sun, she relaxed, something she couldn't do often. She finished the first beer and went to the built-in fridge on the veranda for the second. She saw that the caretaker had noted what kind of beer she drank, Blue Moon Belgian White, and had stocked all of the fridges with it. She loved that man!

Her phone buzzed, and she glanced at the display. It was Tracey. She thought about ignoring it, but she'd only keep calling till she got ahold of her, so Sinclair picked it up.

"Hey," she said.

"That really isn't a proper way to answer a phone, you know."

"What were ya lookin' for?" Sinclair asked, purposely using slang to irritate Tracey further.

Tracey sighed, shaking her head. "Never mind. I take it you're home."

"If I wasn't, I wouldn't have been using this phone, Trace…"

"Oh yes, that's right—this is the non–drug dealer phone."

Sinclair didn't respond. For some reason Tracey was spoiling for a fight, and she wasn't in the mood, so she just waited.

"I should be home day after tomorrow," Tracey said. "Will you

5

still be home?"

"Probably," Sinclair said evenly.

"So… what are you doing tonight?" Tracey asked distractedly; one of her colleagues had just walked up, motioning to her that the next meeting was starting.

"Think I'm gonna hit WeHo," Sinclair said, her green eyes sparkling in the setting sun as she waited for Tracey's reaction.

"Oh Lord," Tracey said predictably. "Don't let any of that trash rub off… I mean, any more of that trash, since I'm sure you still have Watts all over you. Don't you dare sleep in our bed before you shower—God only knows what kind of crud is in that dive they gave you for an apartment down there…"

Sinclair listened to the diatribe while drinking her beer and rolling her eyes. "Well, they don't hand out penthouses to the narcs in Watts, babe—that's just for the narcs in Bel Air.".

"Don't get all cunty," Tracey said sharply.

"Then stop being a cunt."

"I have to go."

"See ya," Sinclair said, hanging up immediately and tossing her phone on the table.

"Definitely hitting WeHo tonight."

That night, Catalina stared openmouthed at Sinclair. "You're a girl…" she said, grinning.

Sinclair laughed. "Some days, yeah."

She was dressed in navy blue slacks, a cream tank top, a fitted jacket in varied shades of blue with a silver star pattern, and navy heels. Her long blond hair was loose and hung to her mid-back in a silky curtain. Her makeup was not overdone, but perfect. Catalina was looking at a completely different person from the one she'd tried to arrest in San Diego.

"That's the newest Cavalli," Devin said, smiling as the newcomer walked up.

"Oh Lord," Skyler said, rolling her light green eyes.

"Sinclair, this is Devin James-Boché and her wife, Skyler Boché," Catalina said.

"Love the Cavalli," Devin said as she nodded to Sinclair.

"Thanks," Sinclair said, smiling in return.

"This is my boss," Catalina said. "Jericho Tehrani and her wife, Zoey. Jericho is the head of the division. Jericho, this is Sinclair Christensen—I told you about her, from my San Diego trip."

Jericho nodded, her bright blue eyes taking in the newcomer with interest. "If you fooled Cat, you must be a pretty good narc."

Sinclair grinned. "Didn't take her for a cop either, so she must have been pretty good too in her UC days."

"I had my moments," Cat said.

Later in the evening, after Cat had introduced Sinclair to everyone in the group, Sinclair had gone out to smoke and get some fresh air when she overheard Jet and Quinn discussing soccer.

"Nah, Brazil isn't doing that well this year," Quinn said, shaking her head, "so Jovina's gonna have to give up that Cup dream."

"I think you're wrong—I think they're gonna pull it out," Jet said.

"Who do you think'll take it?" Sinclair asked Quinn.

"I'm thinking Germany."

"And I'm thinking Italy might come back this time," Sinclair said.

"Nah," Quinn said, shaking her head. "So you know soccer?"

"Played a lot in school. I was even on the LAPD team for a while."

"Well, then you need to hang out with us more. We're getting outnumbered by the girls that don't know soccer."

Sinclair grinned. "I just might do that."

Chapter 1

His name was Anthony Bodega and he was a dirtbag, no question about it. Sinclair always felt the need to take a shower after dealing with him. He dripped machismo out of every pore, and it really rankled him that she had flat out told him she didn't do men. Hell, it was the reason she'd adopted the butch persona, so she could avoid pigs like him in this line of work. She had a good back story and a well-developed reputation for being a hot head who would snap and kill people. It made it a bit easier for her to get through to people when she needed to, but Tony wasn't as easy as a lot of them.

Tony Bodega had a well-developed sense of suspicion; it was the reason she'd been so deep undercover for so damned long. She knew if she could get to Tony's supplier, she could take down a large part of the ring that supplied for the LA Crips. She had to remind herself constantly not to get too antsy. If she did, Tony would sense it, and that could easily get her killed.

"Nah, I think we just need to add some more time to that one option," she drawled, her eyes hidden behind sunglasses. They were sitting out on the veranda of Tony's Malibu home.

"You want more time on that one?" he asked, surprised.

Sinclair shrugged. "I got all the time in the world," she said, grinning lazily.

Tony looked thoughtful for a moment, his dark eyes narrowing slightly.

Sinclair held her emotions in check. What she really wanted was for him to have the drugs delivered this week, like he'd planned. But since he'd brought up the problem with supply, she didn't want to jump at the bait and tell him the shipment needed to be on time regardless of supply issues. She knew that was what he was waiting for from her, and she wasn't going to be stupid and fall for it.

"Well, maybe I can bring in my other guy to make up the difference," Tony said offhandedly.

Sinclair shrugged. "Whatever, man. However you want to do things, this is your gig. I'm just the pass through."

Tony nodded, liking that the lesbo wasn't too concerned about the timing. Even if she wouldn't fuck him, he liked her; she didn't sweat shit she didn't need to worry about. She did what she was told and handled what needed to be handled.

Sinclair's phone pinged, and she glanced at the notification, her expression inscrutable.

"I'm gonna go," she said, getting up. "Got some business to handle on the south end."

"Trouble?"

"Not for long," Sinclair said, her grin menacing.

Tony frowned, but nodded. "Just make sure it's clean."

"Always."

Sinclair walked through the Malibu house, nodding to the men standing around, even stopping to take a good, long look at the hot brunette shaking her ass to the music playing. She walked out to the driveway and got into the Go Green 1970 Dodge Challenger, firing it up with a satisfying roar. It always drew a series of cheers and whistles from the guys at the house. Sinclair shook her head and drove off.

She headed back toward LA. The notification she'd received was from her service, telling her she had an important message. She leaned over and unlocked her glove box, reaching for the other phone she kept there. She called the service and waited for her messages, grimacing when they came through. Taking the next off-ramp, she changed direction and headed for the nursing home.

Inside, she smiled at the nurse at the front desk as she pulled the tie out of her hair; her grandfather preferred her hair down.

"He's being difficult again?" Sinclair asked the nurse.

She rolled her eyes. "You know how he is, girl!"

Sinclair sighed loudly. "Yeah, I know. Let me go see what I can do."

"Good luck!" the woman said, shaking her head. The girl was a saint.

Walking into her grandfather's private room, Sinclair glanced around. There were remnants of food on the wall where he'd apparently thrown his breakfast.

"Practicing for the series again, huh?" she said, smiling as she leaned down to kiss her grandfather's cheek.

"They brought me frigging mangos again—I hate that shit!" Abe Christensen said, making a face, his eyes—green like Sinclair's— flashing in annoyance.

"Okay, well, I'll tell them again about how much you abhor those particular fruit-like substances… but Dad, ya gotta stop throwing shit," she said patiently.

"Oh, what're they gonna do? Stop taking my money?"

"They can kick you outta here, and trust me, you don't wanna know what some of those other places look like."

Abe smiled at Sinclair, patting her hand. "Such a good girl," he said. "We're so lucky to have you."

"So work with me, huh?" Sinclair said, smiling at her grandfather.

Abe grimaced. "It's just so irritating that they can't remember one simple thing."

"I'll tell them you're deathly allergic to them," Sinclair said. "Maybe that'll make them remember."

"Did I tell you why I hate mangos?"

"No—why?" Sinclair asked, settling in for one of her grandfather's stories.

"Well, you see, this movie producer, he wanted to get his picture made real bad. So he kept sending me things. Extravagant things! He sent me wine, and liquor, and once he sent me a girl. Yep! A girl! I thought your grandmother was going to go kill him personally. Oh, she was so mad!"

"Oh, I'll bet."

Sinclair's grandmother, Aida, had been a feisty one. She could easily picture the tiny little redhead storming some guy's office with bat in hand.

"So the next thing he does is start sending me these damned fruit baskets. Apple, pears, grapes—you name it, they were in those baskets! And then came the mangos."

"Okay…" Sinclair said, giving her grandfather a sidelong look. "And what was up with the mangos?"

"Well, they were a big deal in those days, you know, 'cause they weren't as easily available like they are now. So I tried one, and they were great! So I was eating them all the time. Little did I know," he said, putting his hand to his stomach, "they have kind of a…" He leaned forward, whispering dramatically. "Laxative effect."

Sinclair laughed. "How many did you eat before you figured that out?"

"Way too many, I can tell ya!" Abe said, laughing too.

By the time they'd calmed down, Sinclair was wiping tears off her cheeks, she'd laughed so hard.

"Do you know how undignified it is for a studio head to… well, go to the head in the middle of a meeting with Clark Gable?" Abe said.

"You didn't!" Sinclair exclaimed, her mouth agape.

"Yep! Big old fart right there in the meeting. I thought we were all going to die!"

That had Sinclair laughing again. Her sides were hurting by the time she left the nursing home an hour later. She'd secured a promise from her grandfather not to throw food anymore. She'd also talked to the home director and informed him that her grandfather was deathly allergic to mangos, and that was the reason he had hurled them away. Fortunately, the director bought her story. She was really good at lying; it was an occupational hazard.

She glanced at her watch; it was three thirty. Making a quick decision, she made her way over to the medical clinic where River worked. She parked in the back alley and texted River that she was out back if she had time. She leaned against her car, smoking a cigarette, her legs crossed at the ankles. River walked out the back door a couple minutes later.

"Hi!" she said.

"Hey," Sinclair said, smiling and leaning over to kiss her.

"Your hair's loose," River said, reaching up to run her fingers through the long blond mane.

"Yeah," Sinclair said, grimacing inwardly. She'd completely forgotten to put it back in the ponytail she usually wore it in; it was a tiny slip, but it was never good to forget her cover. "Hair thing broke," she lied easily.

"I like it," River said, smiling up at her. "I don't usually see it down when you're... well, dressed."

"Mmm," Sinclair murmured, her green eyes sparkling mischievously. "That sounded dangerously like an invitation."

"It's always an invitation—you know that, Sin," River said, winking at her.

Sinclair nodded as she took another drag on her cigarette. "So what time are you done here today?" she asked, glancing around, as she often did.

"Probably about five," River said, searching Sinclair's face. "Are you coming by tonight?"

Sinclair grinned. "Where do I spend most of my time when I'm home?"

River bit her lip. "My place."

"Then why are you asking if I'm coming by?"

"Because I never want to assume you are," River said, sliding her hand up under Sinclair's leather coat, touching her waist.

Sinclair nodded. "Probably best," she said, her tone conciliatory.

River nodded, leaning into Sinclair and looking up at her. "My sister is coming to town next week," she said, her tone changing slightly.

Sinclair nodded, looking down at the ground as she took another drag. "Got it."

"What do you 'got'?"

"That I'll need to stay at my place while she's here."

River grimaced, worried that the situation was going to irritate Sinclair. She pressed her lips together, feeling bad suddenly. "I'm sorry," she said, putting her hands to either side of Sinclair's coat, her head bowed. "It's just that I haven't really told them about you…"

Sinclair put her tongue against her teeth, her eyes flickering with consternation even as she nodded. She wasn't surprised that River hadn't told her family about her, and in the long run it was better that no one knew much about her. Still, it bothered her, and she knew it shouldn't.

"It's fine," she said evenly as she did her best to tamp down on her hurt feelings. "I know it's… Well, I get it."

"I'm sorry," River said, looking up at Sinclair again, her blue eyes reflecting her words.

"Don't worry about it," Sinclair said, leaning down to kiss her again. "I'll probably be out of town anyway."

River took a deep breath. She knew she'd just hurt Sinclair's feelings and felt bad about that. The fact was she had no idea how to explain to her family what Sinclair did for a living. What was she going to tell them? That she was in import/export? Her family was affiliated with law enforcement; River was afraid they'd decide to investigate Sinclair or something crazy like that.

"River!" yelled a woman from the back door.

Sinclair leaned around to look at her. She was heavy-set and brown-haired, standing there with her hands on her hips. Sinclair recognized her as the head nurse at the clinic.

"She really doesn't like me," she said, grinning.

River smiled up at her. "She doesn't know you."

"Oh, she knows enough. That's why she doesn't like me." Sinclair finished her cigarette and dropped it to stub it out with a booted foot. She glanced back up at the woman, who was still staring at them. "Quick, kiss me and get back in there before she comes out here to kick my ass," Sinclair said, putting her hands to River's hips and pulling her in to kiss her.

River slid her arms around Sinclair's neck, kissing her back, grasping at two handfuls of Sinclair's hair, thoroughly enjoying the feel of it in her hands. Sinclair deepened the kiss, tightening her arms around River's waist. When their lips parted, there was a heated look in River's eyes. Sinclair smiled devilishly.

"You did that on purpose!" River exclaimed.

"Uh-huh," Sinclair said. "Now, just think about that till later."

"You better come by…"

Sinclair smiled. "I'll be there."

"You should see my friend over at the clinic about that," Eddie said as Sinclair did her best not to pass out from the pain.

She'd gotten into it with one of the guys at Tony's place. He had been mouthing off about "lesbos" and all, and Sinclair had had it, so she'd launched herself at him. She'd knocked him to the ground and punched him in the face twice before the other guys pulled her off him. Naturally, because he was embarrassed, the guy pulled a knife and sliced her before she could shake off the other guys and go after him again. Another fight ensued when she wrenched herself out of their grasp.

Eddie, who'd watched the entire thing with fascination, was now trying to be helpful.

"Who's your friend?" Sinclair asked, holding a balled-up rag to her side to try and stop the bleeding.

"Her name's River. She's a nurse, but she'll come to your place so you won't have to go down there and risk running into cops."

"Can you call her for me?"

"Yeah, yeah, sure," Eddie said, ever helpful after the fact.

That night Sinclair opened the door to her department-issued apartment. Seeing the diminutive redhead, she immediately felt a pull at her libido. Not what this is about, *she told herself.*

"Hi, you're River?" Sinclair asked.

"Yes," River said, surprised by the looks of the woman standing in front of her.

"I'm Sinclair," she said, opening the door wider to allow River into the apartment.

River walked inside, noting that the apartment was sparse and fairly tidy. Not like the men's apartments she'd been asked to visit for this same kind of purpose. Then she looked at Sinclair again. The

17

woman was attractive; there was no getting around that. She had a strong jawline, a beautiful face, rich-looking green eyes, and blond hair. She was taller, about five feet eight, with a lean build. River also noticed the sleeve tattoo, a very intricate, detailed design, on one of Sinclair's arms. It added a wild look to her.

"So Eddie said you got cut?" River asked, trying to focus on why she was there rather than the woman.

Sinclair nodded. "Yeah," she said, reaching up and taking off her shirt without preamble, revealing a fairly nice set of abs, a black jog bra, and a bandage that was already bleeding through.

"Oh…" River moved in to carefully touch the bandage. "Nice field dressing there," she said with a grin.

"Thanks. High school first aid class came in handy for once."

River chuckled softly. "Can you please sit down?" she asked, glancing around for a place to sit. It was a studio apartment.

"This okay?" Sinclair said, gesturing to the bed.

"Sure."

They moved to the bed, where River was able to take off the dressing and check the wound.

"It's not too deep," she said, touching the injury as carefully as she could. "I'm going to need to clean it."

Sinclair nodded. "Okay."

"It's going to sting," River said apologetically.

Sinclair grinned. "I didn't imagine it was going to feel good," she said, her eyes sparkling.

River laughed. "I'm sorry."

She took out antiseptic and swabs, and grimaced when Sinclair jumped at the first touch of the swab to the wound. "Sorry," she whispered softly.

It took a little time, but eventually the wound was clean, and she was able to examine it more easily.

"You should probably have stitches."

"Just do what you can," Sinclair said, shaking her head.

"Okay," River said. She'd heard from Eddie that Sinclair wasn't the type to go to the hospital.

"So, your tattoo, does it have some significance?" she asked as she worked.

Sinclair looked down at her arm. "It's Nordic. The top is Fenrir the wolf; the rest is the representation of various Norse gods."

"So I take it you're Scandinavian?" River asked, glancing up at Sinclair.

"I'm a Viking," Sinclair said, her eyes sparkling humorously.

"As evidenced by the wound I'm dealing with here?"

"You should see the other guy," Sinclair said, winking at her.

"He's worse?"

"Well, he's probably got a nasty black eye and a broken jaw."

"Broken jaw?" River asked, widening her eyes.

"Hey, he shouldn't have brought a knife to a fist fight."

"Oh," River said, shocked.

Sinclair grinned. "Did you think I had one too?"

"Well, that seems fair…"

"Yeah, well, trust me—'fair' isn't in that guy's vocabulary. He was being a mouthy son of a bitch about 'lesbos,' and I got tired of it and went after him. He didn't like being bested by a lesbo and pulled a knife."

"And then you broke his jaw?"

"Yep."

"Guess he won't be getting mouthy again anytime soon, will he?" River said, her blue eyes sparkling.

Sinclair smiled. "Nope."

They were both silent for a few minutes while River finished applying butterfly closures to Sinclair's wound.

"So how do you know Eddie?" Sinclair asked.

"Oh, he came into the clinic—he needed a shot..." River said, trailing off.

Sinclair grinned. "For the clap?"

River laughed. "I didn't say that."

"You don't need to. I know he has a thing for hookers."

River pressed her lips together, her eyes shining with humor. "What is it with men and hookers?" she said, shaking her head. "I've never understood that. Why would you want to do something everyone else has already done?"

"Difference between men and women—women need a reason to have sex; men just need a place... to stick it."

"Ugh!" River said, grimacing. "I think I'll stick with women, thanks."

Sinclair canted her head. "You're family?"

"Eddie didn't tell you that?"

"No, he didn't," Sinclair said, shaking her head slowly. "He knows?"

"Oh yeah, he knows. I told him the first time he hit on me."

"Well, you're a lot less obvious."

"I'll bet he hit on you too, though."

"Why do you say that?" Sinclair asked, shifting to lower her arm.

"Because you're... uh..." River stammered, suddenly realizing she'd been about to say, Because you're hot.

Sinclair lowered her head, giving River a sidelong glance. "Because I'm what?" she asked softly.

"Um, well..."

Sinclair smiled, her expression becoming playful. "Well?"

"I think you're good now," River said, moving to stand up.

Sinclair stood at the same time. They were so close. River looked up, seeing the sparkle in those green eyes.

"I..." she stammered, astounded that her body was actually shaking.

"You don't seem to be able to finish that statement," Sinclair said, her voice far too close to River's ear.

"I just need to go before I say something really stupid."

"Like what?"

Sinclair knew she was pushing the girl, and she knew she should back off, but something inside her didn't want to do that. She was ignoring her brain. Her body was saying, Get closer—make her react.

21

Her body was definitely winning the argument.

Sinclair moved imperceptibly closer, and River was fairly certain she could feel her blood pressure rise. She had no idea what it was about this woman that held her enthralled, but there was definitely a loud voice in her head that kept screaming, Tell her!

"Like tell you that you're hot," River said in a rush.

"Just that?" Sinclair whispered, lowering her head to River's ear.

"I need to go," River said, her voice suddenly stronger.

Sinclair knew it was time to back off. She grinned, stepping back and gesturing toward the door.

"What do I owe you?" she asked.

"Nothing," River said, shaking her head as she moved toward the door.

"Wait." Sinclair touched River's arm as she reached into her back pocket for her wallet. She pulled out a hundred dollar bill and put it into River's hand.

"Thank you," she said, nodding.

"This is too much," River said as she tried to hand the money back. "I can't accept this much."

"Keep it."

River shook her head, but Sinclair took a step toward her and River decided she'd better get out of there before anything else happened. She hurried to the door, opening it and rushing out before closing it behind her.

Sinclair stared at the door, her mind reeling at the desire coursing

*through her. It was insane, and she knew it. She'd never been so at-
tracted to anyone, not even Tracey.*

*Two days later, River came out of the clinic after her shift to find Sin-
clair leaning against a bright green muscle car with black racing stripes
right in front. She was smoking a cigarette with her legs crossed at the
ankles. She wore jeans, black boots, and a plain black muscle T-shirt,
her sleeve tattoo on full display.*

"What are you doing here?" River asked warily.

"I thought I'd try this the old-fashioned way."

*"And which way is that?" River asked, her blue eyes widening
slightly.*

"Thought I'd ask you to dinner, see if we can be friends..."

"Friends?"

"Unless you want—"

*"No! Friends is fine," River said, holding her hand up, seeing the
way Sinclair grinned.*

*They went to dinner, and River noticed that Sinclair kept the con-
versation light, steering questions away from what she did. River already had a pretty good idea about what Sinclair did, because she knew
what Eddie did, and who he worked for and what they did. The fact
was, she didn't want to know too much about any of that. It was the
reason she didn't want to get involved with Sinclair, no matter what
her body said every time she looked into those rich green eyes. Unfortunately, dinner didn't serve to dissuade her. Sinclair was an interesting dinner companion. She told River stories of Norse gods and legends.
She pointed out the various parts of her tattoo: which gods they were*

and how they fit into the tapestry of Norse mythology.

"So, what about you?" Sinclair asked at one point.

"What about me?" River said, taking a sip of her wine.

"Why nursing?" Sinclair asked, sitting back in her chair and looking over at her with interest.

River grinned. "Probably because so many in my family needed nursing over the years."

"How many?" Sinclair asked, a smile at her lips.

"Well, I grew up with six brothers, so…"

"Holy shit!" Sinclair exclaimed. "Yeah, that's a lot."

"Do you have brothers and sisters?"

"Nope," Sinclair said, shaking her head. "Only child."

"I see…"

"So what does it take to become a nurse?"

"A degree," River said. "In my case, I only have my ADN."

"What's an ADN?"

"It's an Associate Degree in Nursing. I'm hoping I can go back someday and get my bachelor's or even my master's, but…" She shrugged.

"What's stopping you?"

"Money."

"Can't you get student loans?"

River shook her head. "I don't want to do it that way. I'd rather pay for it as I go."

"But you'd make better money if you had the other degrees,

right?"

"Well, yes, but not such great money that I could afford to pay interest on huge student loan debt."

Sinclair considered that, then nodded. "That makes sense."

"I'll do it someday," River said. "Right now I just have too many bills."

After dinner, Sinclair drove River back to her car, then waited while she got in. The clinic wasn't in the best part of town, so Sinclair wanted to make sure she was safely on her way before she left.

Much to River's chagrin, her old Chevy Cavalier wouldn't start. Sinclair threw her car into park and shut off the engine. She spent the next half an hour trying to see what was wrong with River's car.

"Looks like your starter's gone," she said as she closed the hood, giving the car the sign of the cross and making River grin.

"Well, lovely, that'll be another nice bill," River said, sighing.

"Eh, I can pick you one up and put it in—won't cost ya anything," Sinclair said as she pulled a rag out of her car to wipe her hands off as best she could.

"Oh, Jesus, you're a mess," River said, grimacing. "I'm sorry."

"Did you plan for your starter to go bad?" Sinclair asked, raising an eyebrow at her.

"No, but still... If you'd just gotten away when you dropped me off..."

"You'd be stuck in this neighborhood at ten at night. Yeah, I don't think so. Come on, I'll take you home."

"I can take a cab."

"At this time of night, in this neighborhood?"

"It's not that bad," River said, even as a gunshot sounded out somewhere in the distance.

"Just get in the car," Sinclair said, holding the door to the Challenger open.

"If you insist," River said, grimacing dramatically, making Sinclair chuckle as she shut the door behind her and walked around to the other side.

Ten minutes later they were sitting in front of River's apartment building.

"Thank you," River said. "For dinner, for trying to fix my car... and then the ride."

Sinclair smiled. "Seems to me like you owe me another dinner for all that..."

River gave her a narrowed look. "It does, does it?" she asked, grinning in spite of herself.

"I cut myself on your car," Sinclair said, holding up her arm.

"Oh..." River said, reaching for Sinclair's arm.

"I'm fine," Sinclair said, grinning as she held her arm away.

"Let me see it."

"No, 'cause you'll want to clean it, and I'm not going through that again," Sinclair said as she moved back, holding her arm aloft.

"What is your last name?" River asked, surprising Sinclair.

"Ryerson. Why?"

"So I could say, 'Sinclair Ryerson, let me see your arm!'" River said, lunging for Sinclair's arm again.

Predictably, she ended up against Sinclair's chest, as Sinclair had moved her arm out of her reach yet again. Sinclair chuckled. She raised an eyebrow, knowing full well that she could take advantage of the situation, but something stopped her. River looked up at her, moving slowly back. When she touched Sinclair's hip, however, she felt a wetness. Glancing down at her hand, she saw blood.

"Oh God, Sin, you're bleeding," River said, instantly worried. "You probably dislodged one of the closures. Come up—I can fix it."

River led Sinclair up to her apartment, apologizing profusely for the mess. Sinclair grinned, shaking her head. River led her over to a kitchen chair, pulling it out and sitting her down.

"I'll be right back," she said.

While River was gone, Sinclair gazed around the kitchen. River had all the proper accoutrements, even pots and pans hanging on a rack above the stove.

"You look like you actually cook," Sinclair commented when River walked back into the kitchen.

"I do—don't you?"

Sinclair grinned. "Not if I want it to be edible."

"Oh, my mom was fairly adamant that all women should know how to cook," River said, smiling. She gestured to Sinclair's side. "Okay, let's see it."

Sinclair removed her shirt. River found that she once again had a very visceral reaction to seeing Sinclair's torso. Then she looked at her side.

"Oh God. Yeah, you ripped a couple. Oh, honey," she said, using the endearment without thinking, even as she touched the spot gently.

27

"You bled a lot. It might be easier if you just shower to get off all the dried blood—it might hurt less, plus it'll loosen up those closures so I can replace them."

Sinclair stared at her for a long moment, then nodded. "Okay."

River led her into her bathroom, handing her towels and pointing to the soap.

"Don't go too crazy scrubbing, just really gentle, okay? I don't want you to bleed more."

"Okay," Sinclair said, grinning in amusement at the entire situation.

"Stop that," River said, doing her best not to grin too.

It seemed that Fate kept pushing them together, even when they were trying to avoid it.

Sinclair spent twenty minutes in the shower, debating turning the water to cold so she could get the itch of desire out of her body. When she finally felt like she could control herself, she turned off the water and climbed out, hissing as she shifted the wrong way and the movement pulled at the remaining closures.

"You okay?" River asked from the hallway outside.

"Yeah," Sinclair said as she dried off. She pulled her underwear and pants back on carefully, and then her jog bra, doing her best not to move too much.

Despite her best efforts, the cut was bleeding again by the time she was dressed. She walked out of the bathroom with a towel pressed to the injury.

"You're bleeding again," River said.

"Sorry?"

"No, it's okay," River said, shaking her head. "Come on." She took Sinclair back into the kitchen and sat her down.

As she tried to remove the closures, she kept feeling Sinclair jump.

"Are you allergic to any medications?" River asked.

"Uh, penicillin. Why?"

"I'd like to give you a Vicodin to try and make this less painful. Are you okay with that?"

Sinclair nodded. "Sure."

River went to her bathroom and returned with a pill, which she handed to Sinclair. She turned to get some water.

"I'm good," Sinclair said, popping the pill in her mouth and swallowing it.

"Without water?" River asked, making a face.

Sinclair chuckled. "Yeah, I'm really tough like that," she said, winking.

River worked on getting the cut closed up once again; it took almost an hour. As she finally stood up, she could see that Sinclair was half asleep.

"Uh-oh," River said, grimacing.

"Hmm?" Sinclair murmured, opening her eyes again.

"I think the Vicodin made you drowsy. I guess I didn't think about that."

Sinclair shook her head. "It's okay, I'll be alright," she said, moving to stand and wavering slightly.

"Oh yeah, I can see that," River said, grinning as she reached out to steady the other woman. "I think you should just stay here."

Sinclair thought about it for a moment, then nodded. "Okay, I can sleep on the couch…" She trailed off as she realized River didn't have a couch, only chairs. She smiled. "Or in a chair."

River sighed, shaking her head. "No," she said, resigned. "You're going to come sleep in my bed."

"We were avoiding that, weren't we?" Sinclair asked.

Again River sighed. "Well, I was trying to avoid that, but it seems that Fate has other ideas. Come on," she said, starting toward her bedroom. Once inside, she turned back to Sinclair, surveying her.

"You are not wearing those bloody jeans in my bed," she said decidedly.

"You're just trying to get me to take my clothes off," Sinclair said, sounding extremely tired.

"Yes, that's been my plan all along. How did you guess?"

Sinclair chuckled. "Tell me what's acceptable."

"Sit down and take those jeans off," River said, reaching into a drawer and pulling out a tank top. She tossed it to Sinclair. "That should work."

A few minutes later, Sinclair was lying on the bed, asleep. River went about clearing up the medical supplies in the kitchen then changed for bed, washing her face and brushing out her hair. Walking back into her bedroom, she surveyed Sinclair's sleeping form. Now that her legs were bare, River could see that they were indeed long, and leanly muscled. She looked like a runner. To her amazement, she saw that Sinclair had apparently pulled her hair tie out, because her long *blond hair was fanned out over her pillow. River hadn't realized how long Sinclair's hair was, since it was usually pulled back and completely up.*

Lying down, River pulled the covers up over Sinclair, knowing it would likely get cold in the middle of the night. She didn't run the heater much in the fall, because it cost so much. It took River a little while to go to sleep; her body kept reminding her that Sinclair was lying right there, and if she'd just move over a bit... Finally, she fell asleep.

The next morning, however, River woke to realize that her body had decided for her to get closer to Sinclair. She lay completely still, pressed close to the other woman. Sinclair was lying on her right side, the uninjured side, her arm extended; River felt it under her neck and, opening her eyes, realized she was facing the blonde. Then she realized that her own hand was on Sinclair's waist.

River sternly reminded her body that she was avoiding getting involved with this woman for good reason. It didn't matter. As soon as she felt Sinclair stir, she looked up and saw the most beautiful green eyes staring down at her with the most mischievous glint in them she'd ever seen. Her body begged for her to do something about that.

Sinclair gazed down at River, seeing the look in her eyes, and she knew without a doubt that the girl was having just as much trouble talking her body out of this insanity as she was. She knew she should move away—she knew she should get up out of that bed—but her body just wouldn't listen to her orders.

"So..." River said, trying to find anything she could to distract herself.

"So," Sinclair repeated wryly.

River laughed softly at the look in her eyes. "Okay, so maybe we should just kiss and get it over with. It'll remove the mystery, you know…"

"The mystery," Sinclair said speculatively.

"Yeah, you know how you build things up in your head, imagining something, and in reality it's not that big a deal?"

Sinclair nodded slowly, her expression purposefully blank. "So we should just kiss and get it over with?" she said, her tone reflecting her skepticism.

"Right, because it's bound to be less spectacular than we imagine…"

"We're imagining spectacular?"

That pulled River up short; it suddenly occurred to her that she might be the only one with a major craving at that moment. Was Sinclair just toying with her?

"I… We… I thought…"

Sinclair couldn't let her continue. She leaned in, capturing River's mouth with hers. Unfortunately for the "plan," spectacular didn't even come close to describing the fireworks that went off inside River's body. She grasped at Sinclair's waist as she shuddered at the feel of the strength in Sinclair's lips against hers. Sinclair's arm tightened around her as her lips explored River's with exquisite power and sensuality. When Sinclair gathered her closer, their bodies pressing together, River felt like her body had caught fire. She gave up any hope of fighting it.

Never before had Sinclair been so incredibly turned on by a simple kiss—then again, she'd never initiated a kiss before. Her mind and body hummed with the desire to get a reaction from River, and in getting those reactions, her body was becoming electric with absolute *need.*

Reaching down, she pulled off River's shirt and tossed it aside, pushing down the bikini underwear as well. Moving her lips from River's to trail down her neck, Sinclair felt River's hands at her own shirt. Sinclair removed it and then her underwear as quickly as possible, her body craving the closeness of River's skin. When their bodies met again, they both groaned out loud. Sinclair pulled River over her, wanting to feel her, to touch her and feel her react. Sliding her hands over silky-smooth skin, she shuddered as she felt River press closer. Their bodies melded as Sinclair pulled at River's hips, grinding against her and hearing her ragged intake of breath.

"Yes, yes..." River breathed, grasping at Sinclair's shoulders.

Sinclair slid her hand down over River's ass, pulling her closer and feeling the wetness and heat against her. She increased her movements, knowing that was what would excite them both. River's gasp and corresponding moan indicated her excitement. Sinclair shifted so that River was underneath her, continuing to move and press, lowering her head to kiss River's lips hungrily again.

She felt River's hands at her back, grasping and pulling at her. She felt her nails scratch her skin, and it only served to excite her more.

"God... God..." Sinclair chanted, her body screaming for release. But she held on tight, wanting to wait for River. "Come with me..." she finally whispered harshly as she felt her control slipping.

River immediately cried out at the sound of Sinclair's voice and the erotic command. She gasped and moaned over and over again, coming harder than she remembered ever coming in her life. Hearing Sinclair orgasm with her only intensified it. Even after the orgasm passed, she felt Sinclair continuing to move over her, the sensation so sensual, so hot… She felt her body winding up again.

"Please… please…" River heard herself beg.

Sinclair spent the next two hours making love to her until they were both exhausted and completely spent. Afterward, River lay trying to catch her breath, reflecting on how she'd failed spectacularly at avoiding this woman.

Chapter 2

"I'm not used to media liaisons who don't talk," Talon Valois said, looking over at the woman driving. "It's freakin' me out a little bit…"

Parker Gaines grinned mildly. "I'm not usually a media liaison."

"What are you usually?"

"An actual cop," Parker replied, her tone reflecting her ire.

"Media liaisons aren't 'actual cops'?" Talon asked, amused.

Parker glanced over at the young woman. She looked about twenty-two, maybe a little older. She was all movie star, that was for sure, with her rock star outfit of black leather pants, studded T-shirt, and high heeled boots, and her long earrings and black eyeliner. Parker had no idea what she was doing in a car with this kid, other than getting stuck doing a job she hated.

"No, media liaisons aren't actual cops, normally," Parker replied evenly.

Talon turned to lean against the door of the SUV, her eyes on the other woman. To Talon's way of thinking, she had an "all cop all the time" look; she was wearing dark blue BDUs, with a gun strapped to her thigh and a badge on her breast pocket. Her sandy-brown hair was short in the back, only down to her collar, but the top was longer, pulled back in a ponytail. She wasn't wearing any makeup that Talon could detect. She was definitely butch, but Talon didn't know for sure that she was gay. She found that she was curious though.

As a fairly famous movie star, Talon Valois was used to people falling all over themselves to talk to her. This woman hadn't said more than two words, nor stared at her for more than a moment since they'd met half an hour before. It didn't seem pointed—it just seemed that this woman was the quiet type—but Talon was used to more dynamic people in the position Parker was obviously filling in for at that moment. Talon had never worked with DOJ before, so she had no idea who the normal media liaison was. She did know that the silence was driving her crazy though.

"So when you're not stuck with movie stars, what do you normally do?" Talon asked, her voice reflecting her amusement.

Parker narrowed her eyes slightly; this girl was bound and determined to have a conversation. Once again, she cursed LA traffic for making what should have been a thirty-minute trip take an hour and counting.

"I'm a K9 officer for narcotics," she said.

"So why are you stuck with me?" Talon asked.

"Because I apparently wronged my SAC in a past life."

Talon laughed, not altogether sure that Parker hadn't been completely serious.

The girl's laugh was rather infectious, and Parker found herself grinning at the sound of it.

"Careful," Talon said, reaching out to touch Parker's arm. "That was really damned close to a smile. I wouldn't want you to hurt yourself."

Parker shook her head, rolling her eyes.

They were both silent again for a few minutes, then Talon felt like she had to ask, "So, why are you really stuck doing this job if it's not what you're supposed to be doing?"

Parker blew her breath out, having hoped the girl was out of questions, or had at least gotten the idea that Parker didn't want to talk. No such luck.

"I was injured, so I'm on light duty," she explained as simply as possible.

"What happened?" Talon asked, her green eyes completely guileless.

Parker hesitated, thinking the girl had no concept of boundaries. Finally she shrugged. "I was shot."

"Yikes!" Talon exclaimed. "But you're okay?"

"Apparently okay enough to do this," Parker said mildly.

"So what happens with your dog during this time?"

Parker glanced over at her, thinking the kid needed a filter in the worst way. "He was hurt too."

"Oh shit, is he okay?" Talon asked, her expression so worried that Parker felt a little bit of her ire ebb.

She nodded. "But they retired him, so he lives with me now."

"Well, that's good, I guess... but still, that must really suck."

"It does."

"So, once you get back to your actual job, what happens?"

Parker blew her breath out. Part of her wanted to tell the girl to just mind her own business, but the half that knew she'd get into deep shit with Rayden for doing that knew better.

"I'll get a new dog."

Talon nodded. "So will you be working with Kai Temple for that?"

Parker glanced over at Talon sharply. "How do you know about Kai Temple?"

Talon grinned, pleased to have surprised the stoic cop. "Well, I'm working on a new movie with Legend Azaria, and since it's about one of the members of her group, I've been hanging out with all of them. Kai is part of the group."

Parker nodded slowly, accepting that answer but still a bit surprised.

She knew that Rayden, her boss, had a group of women she hung out with regularly. She also knew that it was how Kai Temple had gotten involved with the department, by providing trained K9s at a much cheaper rate than dogs bred strictly for the purpose of K9 work. Rayden had recently invited Parker to come meet some of her friends for a drink at the local bar, but Parker wasn't sure she was ready to be sociable yet.

She'd joined the department six months before, having been a K9 officer for the LA sheriff's office for many years. When DOJ had begun a K9 program, Jericho Tehrani had reached out to many officers to see if they'd be interested in working for DOJ in their current capacity. At first Parker hadn't been interested in changing departments, but that had changed six months ago.

"So you're going to be working with Kai, right?" Talon prodded.

Parker nodded. "Yes."

"So do you ever hang out with the group?"

Parker looked over at the girl, perplexed as to why she was asking that.

"I mean…" Talon began, then realized she was probably pushing her luck; she didn't even know if the woman was gay. "Well…" She faltered again; there was no real way out of the question.

Parker noted that Talon suddenly looked distinctly uncomfortable, and couldn't help but grin.

"Back yourself into a corner there, petite fille?" she said.

"What did you call me?" Talon asked, looking curious.

"Sorry," Parker said, shaking her head. "High school French coming out. I guess I assumed you are French, with a last name like Valois."

"I am," Talon said. "But I don't speak it, much to my grand-mère's chagrin."

Parker nodded.

"So what did you call me?" Talon asked doggedly.

Parker chuckled. "I called you *little girl*. Which sounds worse in English than it does in French," she added, grimacing slightly.

"How so?" Talon asked, curious how this woman would see it.

"Well, in English it sounds condescending."

"And you didn't mean to be condescending?" Talon asked, raising one black eyebrow.

Parker stared back at the girl for a long moment, looking like she was assessing the answer to that question. Finally she shook her head.

"No," she said. "I was just poking at you for assuming I'm gay and would hang out with Kai and her group."

Talon licked her lips nervously, wondering if she'd offended the woman.

"I'm sorry," she said, looking like she truly was. "It was wrong of me to assume that. I guess I was hoping you were."

"Why would you hope I was?" Parker asked, completely shocked.

Talon grinned impishly. "'Cause I always want strong, beautiful women in power to be gay," she said with a shrug.

Parker's expression flickered between surprise and amusement.

"So are you?" Talon asked, realizing that Parker had never said one way or the other.

Parker didn't reply. Instead she pulled up to the location they were scouting for the fundraiser event that they had been tasked with arranging. When Parker got out of the car without answering, Talon started to laugh, shaking her head.

Getting out of the car, she looked over at her. "You're not going to tell me?"

"What difference does it make?"

Talon grinned, her green eyes sparkling. "'Cause now I'm really curious."

"Curiosity is a healthy thing," Parker said, then gestured for Talon to precede her into the building.

"Not for me, it's not," Talon said, widening her eyes.

Parker appeared unmoved by the comment, merely looking back at her.

Talon shook her head and walked into the venue.

The fundraiser was for the local community shelter for women and children. It was something Midnight wanted DOJ to participate in, and it was a charity that Talon had been a major spokesperson for, which was why they were on the project together. Parker had been surprised to hear that a movie star of Talon Valois' caliber was taking the time to participate in the planning of the event.

"So you're really in at this level?" Parker asked as they got ready to leave, after having talked to the event manager.

"I'm kind of a control freak," Talon said. She grinned engagingly. "It's a childhood trauma kind of thing."

Parker chuckled. "Well, I'm half lost on this whole thing, so…" she admitted, trailing off as she shrugged.

"I'll help ya out—I'm really good with virgins," Talon said, giving her a sly look. "Now just tell me if you're gay or not."

Parker stared back at her, her blue eyes sparkling, then shrugged and walked out the door of the venue.

Talon stared after her, shaking her head. This was becoming a game now.

"You're going to force me to drastic action if you won't answer my question," she said when they were back in the car.

Parker's lips curled sardonically. "I'll take my chances."

"You say that now…" Talon said as she shook her head, her tone sing-song.

Parker made no comment, just nodded.

A week later, Talon knocked on Parker's office door. Parker called for her to come in, and Talon stepped inside.

Parker glanced at the girl and was surprised. She looked quite different than she had before. This time she wore a very feminine-looking cowl-neck sweater in moss green, with black leggings and knee-length lace-up heeled boots. Her makeup was soft and feminine as well, and her hair was curled attractively, falling just past her shoulders.

Talon saw the surprise flicker over Parker's face, and was once again pleased to have shocked the woman.

"Hi," she said, smiling brightly.

"Hello," Parker said, gesturing to the chair in front of her desk.

Talon sat down, crossing her legs, her gaze roaming over Parker's office. Nothing in the room helped her out with the "Are you gay?" question. There were no pictures of women or men. There was a photo of Parker and what must be her dog, a black German Shepherd.

"What's his name?" Talon asked, nodding toward the picture.

Parker grinned. "Bandit."

"Is he really okay?"

"Yeah," Parker said. "But he can't run like he did—his leg was injured."

"How did they manage to hit both of you?"

"Shotgun blast," Parker said simply.

"That's crazy…" Talon breathed, shaking her head. "I'm really glad you're both okay."

Parker's lips twitched, her expression once again surprised, but she inclined her head.

"That surprises you," Talon said. "Why?"

Parker's lips curled. "Just not what I expected."

"From me or from anyone?"

Parker didn't answer, just shook her head.

"You have a bad habit of not answering questions," Talon observed.

"I've heard that."

Talon stared back at Parker for a long moment; the woman was like Fort Knox. It was becoming a major challenge, and that was never a good thing.

"So," Parker said eventually, turning to her computer even as she picked up an orange and began peeling it. She opened a spreadsheet. "Here are our options," she said, pointing to the screen and eating a section of orange. "Sorry," she added when Talon looked at her strangely. "Haven't had lunch."

"And that's lunch?"

"It is today."

Talon got up and walked around the desk to perch on Parker's chair, looking at the screen.

Parker did her best not to notice that the woman smelled fantastic. *I would have found her attractive when I was still alive*, she thought grimly.

Leaning forward, Parker pointed to the first location. "This one I think we can eliminate. They were a bit small and they had way too many restrictions."

Talon nodded. "I agree with you on that one. We don't want to have to limit our attendance on this because of the venue." She picked up a section of orange and popped it into her mouth.

"Exactly," Parker said, shaking her head at the girl. She definitely wasn't shy. "This second one is a challenge, though, because they want a deposit, and I'm not sure the department can front that much without the services being done."

"That's not a problem. I'm paying for the venue, so I can do whatever they need," Talon said, shaking her head.

"You're…" Parker began, shocked.

"What?"

"You're paying for the venue?"

Talon grinned. "Have I impressed you now?"

"Maybe…" Parker said noncommittally.

Talon smiled. "Well, I wasn't trying. That's been my plan all along."

"That's awfully generous of you."

"I can afford it, trust me."

"Okay…"

They discussed the other venues and decided to go back and look at three of them during actual events so they could check them out in their proper form. They set a date to meet up. Parker was curious who would show up this time.

She wasn't disappointed. This time Talon was both feminine and masculine in a very well-cut black suit with high heels, her makeup done in such a way that it was hard to tell she had any on—but she looked amazing. Her hair was up in a twist, with a wicked, high-curved style in the front. Parker shook her head.

"What?" Talon asked, smiling widely.

"Can't ever tell who's gonna show up."

"That's the plan," Talon said, her green eyes sparkling. "You look nice," she added, admiring the navy blue slacks and the crisp white shirt with a rich blue paisley vest and tie. What surprised Talon more was that Parker's shirt sleeves were rolled up to reveal tattoos on her arms—so she did have a bit of a wild side.

"Thanks," Parker said, smiling almost shyly. "We can take my car if you'd like."

"Afraid to let me drive?" Talon asked, grinning.

"A little bit," Parker said, grinning too. "I've seen that blue rocket you drive."

"It's a Lamborghini—it's a requirement that you drive it fast."

"That's what I was afraid of. My car is just out front."

Talon smiled. "If you insist."

They walked out of Talon's building, and she gave a low whistle at the classic muscle car that sat in front. She ran her hand along the front fender appreciatively.

"What is this?" she asked.

"It's a '68 Cougar."

"Nice…"

Parker opened the passenger door for Talon. She got inside, looking around the interior of the vehicle. Everything was polished chrome and leather. The car was in pristine, fully restored condition.

As Parker got in on the other side, her phone rang. She put her Bluetooth in her ear and answered as she started the car. Talon could only hear Parker's side of the conversation, but she saw the name Chelle on the display of the phone.

"Hello? Oh, hi. No. Yes, I got it. Uh-huh. Okay… No, I'm fine." Her expression became pained then. "No, he's fine. No, you can't. Because—" Her voice broke slightly as she shook her head. "No, you can't, because you gave that up when you chose this," she said, her voice stronger, with a touch of anger. "I gotta go. No, I gotta go."

With that, Parker disconnected the call.

Talon could see that she was upset. She didn't hesitate; she reached over, taking Parker's hand.

"Are you okay?"

Parker glanced over. She looked pensive, but she nodded.

Talon grinned. "So I guess that answers my question, huh?"

"Probably," Parker said, looking chagrined.

"So… girlfriend?" Talon asked, gesturing toward the phone.

"Wife," Parker said. "Of twenty years."

"Wow…" Talon said, her eyes wide.

"Yeah, for all the good that did me."

"I take it you're getting divorced?" Talon asked tentatively.

"Yep."

"You don't look happy about that. I'm sorry."

Parker shook her head. "It is what it is."

Talon nodded, looking pained.

They were both silent for a few minutes as Parker drove, getting on the freeway to head toward the first venue.

"You know, if you don't want to do this tonight..." Talon began.

"It's fine," Parker said, glancing over at her. "We need to get something booked before we run out of time."

Talon nodded. "But I could just take a look at them—you don't have to be dragged along."

Parker reached over, touching Talon's leg. "I'm fine. Let's just do this, okay?"

Talon put her hand over Parker's, nodding. "Okay."

She found she was disappointed when Parker put her hand back on the steering wheel. Once again they were silent, then Talon looked over at Parker.

"I think you need to blow off some steam," she said, grinning wickedly.

"You do, huh?" Parker asked mildly. "And what would you propose I do to do that?"

"Have you ever been skydiving?"

"Uh, no," Parker said, grinning. "I was a submariner—we don't jump out of perfectly good airplanes."

"Really?" Talon asked. "But you'll get on a boat that's going to sink on purpose?"

Parker laughed. "You must have some ex-military in your family."

"I've been around ex-military a lot."

47

Parker nodded.

"Okay, so no skydiving," Talon said. "Have you ever driven a race car?"

"Every day," Parker replied, gunning the 427 engine to prove her point.

"Okay, but I mean like actual race cars on a track."

"Nope, can't say I have."

"Then that's what we need to do."

"We do?" Parker asked.

"Yep," Talon said. "I'll plan it. How about next Saturday? I'll invite the girls so it won't seem like a date or anything. It'll give you a chance to meet more of them."

Parker glanced over at her. "Why are you doing this?"

"Because I like you," Talon said simply.

Parker stared at her, assessing.

"Jesus, hasn't anyone ever done anything nice for you?" Talon asked.

"People who know me really well… maybe."

"So, I guess I'm weird," Talon said, grinning.

"That's a safe statement."

Talon's mouth dropped open, and then she saw the sparkle of humor in Parker's eyes.

"Hey… that was like a joke," she said.

"Yeah, *like* one."

Talon laughed. "There is a sense of humor in there, I just have to find it."

"Great…" Parker said, sounding anything but enthusiastic.

"So you were in the Navy?" Talon asked.

"Yep," Parker said, taking the exit they needed.

"For how long?"

"Eight years."

"And on a sub? What did you do?"

"Yes, on a sub, and I was a navigator."

"Cool," Talon said. "So did you join when you were eighteen?"

"Twenty. Got my degree first so I could go in as an officer."

"You were an officer?"

"Just a lieutenant when I discharged."

"Just?" Talon said, looking at her pointedly.

Parker shrugged. "Yeah, just."

"And you got a degree when you were twenty? What level?"

"Bachelor's."

"In?"

"Poli-sci."

Talon nodded, impressed. "Wait, how did you get a four-year degree in two years?"

"Well, I actually got my GED when I was sixteen and a half, so technically it was three and a half years."

"GED?"

Parker nodded. "Yeah. My dad was really sick, so I had to quit school when I was fifteen to take care of him. I ended up getting my GED because he didn't want me to be a dropout."

Talon was once again surprised. "So... did he get better?" she asked hesitantly.

"No," Parker said. "He passed when I was seventeen."

"Oh, God, I'm sorry," Talon said, shaking her head. "What about your mother?"

"She's never really been in the picture; it was just me and my dad since I was about two."

Talon shook her head again. "That's really rough."

Talon had issues with her parents, but she'd never been without them, and certainly hadn't gone through what Parker apparently had.

Parker shrugged. "It was what it was. My dad was the reason I joined the Navy in the first place. He'd been Navy."

They were both quiet for a couple of minutes.

"So you said you were married for twenty years—when did you meet her?" Talon asked.

Parker looked a little more circumspect, and Talon knew she was treading too close to sensitive waters.

"When I was twenty-five. On my birthday, actually."

Talon nodded. "So you got married before you were even out of the Navy?"

"Well, as married as we could be at that point."

"Oh, yeah. True."

"We got legally married in Massachusetts in 2003, once that was allowed," Parker said, wondering why she was telling Talon all of this.

Talon nodded.

They pulled up to the venue then, and Parker got out of the car. Talon got out as well, smiling at Parker, who'd been walking around to open her door.

"Not a total girlie girl—you don't have to open my door for me," she said.

Parker pursed her lips, nodding as she realized it was a habit of hers. Chelle was a total girlie girl, and Parker had liked that about her.

Parker knew she was taking chances, hitting a gay bar while she was on leave in San Diego, but she figured if she saw anyone she knew there, they'd be in the same boat as her. It was her birthday, after all—why shouldn't she be allowed to celebrate her way?

She'd been outside smoking when a very pretty blonde walked up, taking out a cigarette.

"Do you have a light," the blonde asked, smiling shyly.

"Sure," Parker said, pulling her lighter out.

"Thanks," the girl said, checking Parker out as she did. "I've never seen you here before."

Parker grinned. "I'm not from San Diego."

"Where are you from?" the girl asked. "I'm Chelle, by the way— it's short for Michelle."

"Parker."

"Parker?"

"Yeah," she replied, lighting another cigarette. "My dad wanted a boy. He was in love with the name by the time he got a girl."

"Oh," Chelle said, smiling. "It's actually pretty cool."

"Thanks," Parker said, leaning back against the wall, crossing her legs at the ankles.

"So where are you from?" Chelle asked again.

"Oh, sorry," Parker said. "LA, normally."

"So what are you doing way down here?"

"My boat's in dock."

"Your boat?" Chelle asked, looking somewhere between confused and impressed.

Parker chuckled, shaking her head. "I'm in the Navy."

"Oh!" Chelle said. "Aren't you taking a big risk, coming here?"

Parker nodded. "Yeah, but I figure if anyone from my boat is here, then we're both guilty, so…"

"Well, yeah, with that stupid Don't Ask, Don't Tell shit," Chelle said angrily.

"That's a safe statement," Parker said, grinning.

Chelle laughed softly. "Sorry, I just hate the way groups like the military handle things they don't understand."

"If you can't shoot it or blow it up, run away from it."

"Yeah…" Chelle said, smiling. "So you're here alone?"

Parker nodded. "I'm celebrating."

"What are you celebrating?"

"My birthday."

"Ohhh… Happy birthday."

Parker grinned. "Thanks."

"How old are you today?"

"Twenty-five."

"I just turned twenty-one a week ago."

"Well, happy belated birthday," Parker said. *"You just turned twenty-one, but you've been coming here long enough to know I've never been here?"* she asked, her look sly.

Chelle grinned mischievously. "Fake ID."

Parker laughed. "For shame!"

"A girl's gotta do what a girl's gotta do…"

Parker shook her head, grinning.

"So are you going to let me buy you a drink for your birthday?" *Chelle asked.*

"I think I might be able to do that."

They spent the rest of the night at the bar together, and Chelle invited her back to her apartment, which she shared with two other girls. In Chelle's room, she immediately began kissing Parker, and they made love shortly after that. Afterward they lay together, Chelle against Parker's side, tracing patterns on her stomach with her finger.

"I didn't even ask before," she said, glancing up at Parker. *"Are you stationed here in San Diego?"*

"No," Parker said, shaking her head. *"I'm up at SeaTac in Washington."*

"SeaTac?"

"Seattle Tacoma."

"Oh," Chelle said, looking crestfallen. *"So why are you in San Diego?"*

53

"There were some things we needed for the boat, so we're here for a bit."

Chelle nodded, snuggling closer. Parker stayed that night, because Chelle didn't want her to leave.

They ended up spending the better part of the next six months together. Whenever Parker wasn't working, she was at Chelle's apartment. Fortunately, Chelle's roomates were also gay, and really liked Parker, because she made Chelle happy, so it wasn't an issue for them.

One day, Parker showed up at Chelle's job unexpectedly, asking if she could go to lunch a little early. Chelle got an okay from her boss, and they headed out.

They went to a restaurant nearby. Chelle noticed that Parker was smoking a lot, and that usually meant she was stressed about something.

"What's going on, babe?" she asked, afraid that somehow Parker had been caught and was getting kicked out of the Navy.

"We just got orders."

"For?" Chelle asked, relieved that it wasn't what she'd thought.

"WESTPAC."

"Which is what?"

"It's basically a deployment for six months," Parker said.

Chelle took a deep breath, blowing it out in a sigh. "And you probably won't be coming back here after, will you?"

"Probably not," Parker said, her expression serious.

"When do you go?" Chelle asked, having now lost all interest in her food, which had just arrived.

"About two weeks," Parker said, her blue eyes searching Chelle's face. "Would you take a trip up to Seattle with me?"

"Before you go?"

Parker nodded. "Yeah."

"I'd love to," Chelle said, smiling. "I've never been anywhere out of San Diego, except TJ, and that doesn't really count."

They flew up to Seattle, and Parker took Chelle to the house she'd bought in Everett, Washington. It was a small Craftsman-style house. Chelle was very taken with it right away, with its beautiful wood trim and the fireplaces built of stone.

"It still needs work," Parker said. "But I've been doing what I can when I'm off shift."

"I like it," Chelle said, running her hand reverently over the rich redwood. "It's really beautiful."

Parker smiled, glad that Chelle seemed to share her love of the old place. She showed her around the rest of the house, and then took her to the master bedroom. The room was painted a light shade of sage green, and had the wide redwood trim around the doors and windows. The furniture matched the colors of the wood, and was obviously antique, but solidly built. The bed was a sleigh style with heavy head and foot boards. The bedding was shades of navy blue and gray. Chelle walked over to the bed, running her hand over the comforter, looking at Parker pointedly.

"Trying to tell me something?" Parker asked, grinning.

Chelle smiled. "Trying to tell you to get over here."

Parker walked over and Chelle wrapped her arms around her

neck, pulling her head down to kiss her. Within minutes they were on the bed, making love. It was a nice beginning to their trip.

In the following days, Parker showed Chelle around the area. She drove her up to the Bangor sub base to show her generally where she worked, but didn't dare to take her onto the base.

Their last night in Washington, they lay in bed together after having made love. Chelle rested her head on Parker's chest, her hand, as usual, tracing patterns on Parker's stomach.

"I'm going to miss you," Chelle said softly.

Parker gave her shoulder a squeeze. "I'll miss you too," she said, turning to kiss Chelle's forehead tenderly.

"It sucks that I'm not even going to see you when you get back."

"I was wondering about that…"

"About what?" Chelle said, moving to look up at Parker.

"About when I get back."

"What were you wondering about it?" Chelle asked, obviously confused.

"Whether you'd be willing to be here when I got back…" Parker said, trailing off as she canted her head to look down at Chelle.

"Are you asking me to move up here?"

"I'm asking you to move in here," Parker clarified.

"I…" Chelle looked shocked. "Wow…"

"Is it too much to ask?" Parker said, worried.

Chelle looked contemplative for a moment, then glanced up at Parker. "I'd love to move in here with you," she said, smiling warmly and moving to kiss Parker deeply.

Parker left for her WESTPAC two days later, and when she returned after six months, Chelle had not only moved into the house in Everett, she'd started working on the projects that Parker had talked about. They made a great team.

Chapter 3

Sinclair knew immediately that Tracey was home when she walked into the house in Bel Air. The air was different, like there was less of it. She'd dragged herself out of River's bed that morning, dreading coming home, but she needed to do a few reports and check in at the office before her commander climbed down her neck again.

She reached into the fridge for a beer, glancing at the clock. It was noon. She knew she was going to hear it from Tracey anyway—might as well be fortified when she did. Removing the cap, she resisted the urge to toss it on the counter—no sense in causing another fight. She threw the cap into the trash can and made her way to the back of the house, walking out onto the patio and looking at the view of Los Angeles far below. Sitting down, she lifted the beer to her lips and stared at the city.

"It's noon and you're drinking?" Tracey's voice started her awake. Apparently she'd drifted off.

"It's five o'clock somewhere," Sinclair said, grinning as she picked up the beer and finished the bottle, then stood up.

"So this job is turning you into an alcoholic," Tracey observed, her already thin-lipped mouth thinner with disapproval.

Why hadn't Sinclair noticed before how thin Tracey's lips were? Or was that compared to River's full, kissable lips? She wasn't sure.

"God, lighten up, will ya?" she said, moving past Tracey and heading into the house.

"I do hope you're going to shower," Tracey commented as she followed her back inside.

"I do hope you're going to stop bitching at me at some point," Sinclair muttered as she walked into their bedroom, taking off her jacket and tossing it on the bed.

"What did you say? Jesus! Not on the bed!"

Sinclair didn't comment, simply stripped down and walked into the bathroom. Twenty minutes later she climbed out of the shower and grabbed a towel, grimacing as she rubbed the latest bruise too hard. When she went back into the bedroom, Tracey was sitting at the desk, on the computer.

"What did you manage to do to yourself this time?" Tracey asked, raising an eyebrow at the cut on Sinclair's side.

"I stopped a fist with my side," Sinclair said as she got dressed, pulling on jeans and an LAPD sweatshirt then sitting down to put her boots on.

"Why can't you just answer a question?"

Sinclair glanced back at Tracey, seeing the really butch woman she'd married, who was ten years her senior, and comparing her to the twenty-five-year-old whose bed she'd left that morning. Tracey came out way behind, and not just in the looks and sex appeal department. Tracey had become more and more nagging and downright mean in the last two years, and Sinclair was more than happy to have her gone all the time.

"Because I don't honestly think you care what happened, and if I tell you it'll just give you more ammunition to use as to why I should quit my job and be your little house bunny."

Tracey stared back at her for a long minute, her face unreadable. It was her negotiator's face; Sinclair recognized it well.

"You think I don't care about you?" Tracey asked, her brown eyes reflecting surprise.

"I think you care more about what you want than you care about me."

"Why would I ask what had happened if I didn't care?"

Sinclair looked back at her, trying to decide if Tracey was actually hurt by the accusation or if she was just trying to negotiate her point. Then it clicked.

"Why wouldn't you show real concern and touch me instead of sitting all the way the hell over there and asking what I 'managed' to do to myself 'this time'?"

"Clair…" Tracey began, her tone softening, though she still didn't move from the desk and her eyes kept straying back to the computer.

"I gotta go to the office," Sinclair said, shaking her head. "I'll see you later."

Tracey glanced up as Sinclair walked out of the room. She narrowed her eyes slightly, seeing once again how different Sinclair looked now compared to how she had when they'd met and married.

Sinclair moved through the crowd, smiling at people she knew and grabbing a glass of champagne off a passing tray. She looked beautiful in a rich emerald gown that nearly matched her eyes. Her long blond hair was curled, silky and shining. She was doing her best to escape a particularly verbose director who insisted on telling her how much she looked like her mother. She headed out to the veranda of the hotel and leaned against the railing, sighing.

"That's an awfully heavy sigh for someone so young and beautiful," came a voice from behind her.

Sinclair turned and saw a woman dressed in a tuxedo, looking very handsome in it, walking toward her. She smiled.

"It was a sigh of relief," she said. "I was successful in my escape."

"Escape of...?"

"From... actually, from a director friend of my parents."

"I see. You don't like talking to directors?" the woman asked, a sparkle in her eye.

"Not when it's endless stories about how I look like my mother, and so on and so forth," Sinclair said, a shadow in her eyes.

The woman moved closer, her expression softening. "I take it that's a tender subject?"

"Very," Sinclair said, blinking to try and hold back the tears that were in her throat suddenly. She wasn't successful.

She was shocked when the woman handed her a handkerchief.

"I didn't think people carried these anymore," Sinclair said, smiling as she used the handkerchief to touch at her eyes.

"Well, some of us are still old school."

"Thankfully," Sinclair said. "I'm Sinclair Christensen."

"Tracey Aramark," the woman said, inclining her head gallantly.

Sinclair grimaced. "And now I've got makeup all over your handkerchief."

"Keep it," Tracey said. "You might need it again if that director finds you," she added, winking.

"Not if you stick with me to hold him off," Sinclair said, smiling hopefully.

"I'd be happy to do just that," Tracey said, and offered Sinclair her arm.

Tracey's gallant ways had won her over easily. It had almost seemed natural when she and Tracey made love the first time. To Sinclair, becoming gay wasn't difficult in the slightest; she let Tracey set the pace of their relationship, and before six months had elapsed they were getting married. It was a whirlwind romance—that's what everyone said. And things were great between them for the first three years. They'd even talked about kids, although Sinclair was a police officer and she wasn't sure how she could be that and get pregnant. That had been the first time Tracey had suggested that she quit the department. It had been the prelude to things to come.

In the garage, Sinclair climbed into her low-slung Mercedes SL550, glancing over at the Challenger, the car she considered her alter-ego. Starting the Mercedes with less of a satisfying roar, but definitely a feeling of power, the smell of leather heady in her nostrils, Sinclair grinned. Music flowed from the speakers; she smiled as she turned it up louder and backed out of the garage.

She sped off along the winding roads that led down to the Sunset Strip, heading east to the LAPD headquarters. She spent four hours in the office, filling out status reports, checking in with her team members, and returning calls. One of the messages was another from

Catalina Roché, asking if she was interested in a position she had coming open. She went on to say that she could request her assistance from LAPD, and since her current case involved a meth lab it would technically cross over. It was a way to ease the transition from LAPD into the Department of Justice. Catalina had already enticed her as much as she could with the opportunity for more freedom on her cases. One thing that was attractive to her was working for Catalina, versus her current supervisor, who was a man and kind of a jerk. Sinclair had done her best to work with him for the last year, since he had taken over her unit, but they just didn't get along at all.

Getting up from her desk and stretching, Sinclair glanced at her watch. It was getting close to four, which mean traffic was going to start to suck. Not that traffic in LA didn't suck all the time, but it got worse in the later hours of the day. After pulling her jacket off her chair and putting her gun at her back, she picked up the reports she'd printed out and took them to her boss's office. Unfortunately, he was there.

"Christensen," he said, his tone already sarcastic. "Nice of you to join us for a moment."

"Sir, the point of deep cover is not to break it too often," Sinclair said evenly.

"That doesn't mean you don't need to check in now and again."

She nodded, even as she turned to leave, and muttered under her breath, "Actually, it does."

She left the building, pausing long enough to light a cigarette outside. Striding across the street, she finished her smoke and got into her car. It took her an hour and half to get home; she cussed halfway there, then finally gave up and cranked her music.

She pulled into her garage at 5:35 p.m. Inside, she dropped her keys into the Imari bowl and went into the kitchen to grab a beer. She headed into the living room and sat down on the couch, then turned on the TV, looking for something to watch. She settled happily on a soccer game.

Tracey found her an hour later, half lying on the couch, drinking her third beer and watching the game. Surveying her wife, Tracey wished for the old days, when Sinclair would never have drunk her beer from a bottle, nor would she be free of makeup, and wouldn't have worn combat boots unless they had heels and went with a cute outfit. It seemed like those days were truly gone sometimes.

"I'm thinking we should get dinner at Spago tonight," Tracey said. "I made a reservation for eight."

Sinclair glanced at her watch; it was almost seven. "Seriously?" she said as she sat up, setting her beer on the coffee table in front of her.

"You like Spago."

"No, you like Spago. I like friggin' pizza."

"Well, how about you get all dressed up and we have a nice dinner for a change?" Tracey asked, her voice exceedingly nice.

Sinclair narrowed her eyes. "Why do I sense that the key part of that sentence is for me to get all dressed up?"

"Is it that hard for you now?"

"It isn't hard," Sinclair said. "It's that you absolutely refuse to accept who I am now."

"I don't understand why you feel the need to take on your undercover persona in your regular life. It's like you're trying to become someone else."

"I'm trying to get comfortable in my own skin, Trace. Why does it bother you so much?"

"Because I'm not attracted to butches, Clair."

"It's that black and white to you?" Sinclair said. "You only love me if I'm femme? So do you actually love me, or do you love the idea of me?"

Tracey didn't answer for a long moment, and to Sinclair that was her answer.

"I just want what we had before," Tracey said.

"And I want to live in the present," Sinclair said.

"Can we please just go have a nice dinner?"

Sinclair stared back at her wife and thought how tired she was of arguing with her. She just wanted some peace. Sighing, she got up off the couch and walked past Tracey toward the bedroom.

Half an hour later she emerged wearing white slacks, a Kobi Halperin embroidered sleeveless blouse in white and various shades of blue, and a fitted white-leather cropped jacket and white heels. Her makeup was perfect and she'd fixed her hair partially up, attractively soft around her face.

Tracey's face lit up when she saw Sinclair. She smiled widely, walking forward and leaning down to kiss her softly on the lips. To Sinclair, it felt like she was wearing a costume, but it made Tracey happy, which meant they didn't get into a wicked fight that evening. They had a nice dinner at Spago. Tracey got to show her beautiful wife off and that made her happy.

Later, Sinclair stood at the sink to take off her makeup, wearing just her white satin bra and matching bikini panties. Tracey walked up behind her, staring at her in the mirror.

"You are so beautiful," she whispered, her hands on Sinclair's waist.

Sinclair glanced at Tracey in the reflection, seeing the look in her eyes. Tracey's hand slid upward, unclasping Sinclair's bra and slipping it off. She then moved her hands down to remove the panties. She took Sinclair's hand, leading her to the bedroom and laying her down on the bed. There she began touching her breasts, kissing her lips, and then sliding her hand down between her legs. Sinclair closed her eyes and thought about what she'd done with River the night before. Only then did she get excited; only then could she come.

Afterward, Tracey lay behind her, her arms around her. Sinclair reached back, touching Tracey's hip, sliding her hand over her slacks and then unhooking the pants and unzipping them, slipping her hand inside. It was almost businesslike, the way she made her wife come; she could practically do it in her sleep. Tracey orgasmed quietly. Sinclair remembered the way River had come for her, and thought about how much she missed the woman already.

Two days later, Sinclair woke up and saw that Tracey was sitting at the desk in the room. She went into the bathroom, and when she emerged she noticed that Tracey was watching her critically.

"You're getting bulky," Tracey said sternly.

"Well, thanks, that's so sweet," Sinclair said, shaking her head as she walked over to pull on her yoga pants.

"You should stop working with that Kai person and just stick to the dance stuff."

"And you should stop trying to tell me what to do," Sinclair said, putting on her jacket and shoes so she could go out to the patio to smoke.

"You're smoking an awful lot lately."

"Gee, I wonder why," Sinclair muttered as she walked out the slider in their bedroom.

Sinclair sat out on the covered patio just off their bedroom, which overlooked the LA skyline. She smoked her way through a number of cigarettes as she thought about how things between her and Tracey had deteriorated.

"Why are you dressed like that?" Tracey asked, seeing the jeans and boots, and the butch-looking tank top, thick-banded watch and wrist band.

"It's for my cover," Sinclair said. "I figure if I look really butch, drug dealers are likely to hassle me less."

"Hassle you?"

"Uh… try to fuck me."

"Jesus, don't use that kind of language. It's so gutter," Tracey said, aghast.

"Okay, so try to have intercourse with me," Sinclair said, laughing. "You know what I mean."

"So you're going to have to stave off male attention on top of everything else?" Tracey asked, looking appalled by the idea.

"Well, that's not technically the job, but men in this arena tend to have little or no respect for women, so…" Sinclair shrugged.

"And why do you want to do this undercover stuff again?"

"Well, I'd like to make a difference in the city we live in."

"And you think you're going to make such a difference that it's going to change something?" Tracey asked mockingly.

Sinclair looked back at her for a long moment, blinking. She was shocked by what Tracey had just said, and it hurt. Turning away, she walked out of the room, taking refuge on the back patio, walking around the pool and leaning on the railing to look out at the city below. She waited for Tracey to come and apologize. She never did. It was the very first crack in their perfect marriage.

Later, another battle ensued over why Sinclair wouldn't attend a studio party with Tracey in three days' time.

"I'm going to be back under by then," Sinclair said.

"And it can't wait?" Tracey's tone belied how unimportant she felt Sinclair's job was compared to what she wanted from her.

"No, it can't wait," Sinclair said, gritting her teeth to keep from yelling. "I have a meeting with one of the mid-level dealers and I need to make sure I'm ready."

"Ready?" Tracey said, as if she couldn't fathom how difficult it could be to be "ready" to meet a drug dealer.

"I need to have all my information lined up, and I need to make sure I know... Fuck, why am I explaining myself to you anyway? Either way, I'm not going to the party, so get over it."

"You are my wife. It's your job as my wife to be with me for big things like this. I need you there."

"My job?" Sinclair said, dumbfounded. "Did you just say it's my job to do this for you?"

"Yes," Tracey said, not one to back off once she'd said something, whether it was completely ridiculous or not.

Sinclair laughed, shaking her head. "You've got to be fucking kidding me right now, right?"

"Don't use that kind of language," Tracey snapped.

"Don't fucking tell me what to do!" Sinclair screamed back.

"You're acting like a child."

"Well, then let me throw a temper tantrum and get the fuck out of here."

She proceeded to yank on her jeans, shoved her feet into her boots, and grabbed her jacket, cigarettes, lighter, and the keys to the Challenger.

"You're not supposed to go back for two more days!" Tracey yelled. She knew that if Sinclair was taking the Challenger, she was going back to her cover.

"New fucking plan!" Sinclair shouted back as she slammed out the garage door.

The Challenger started with a roar a minute later. Tracey made it out to the garage just as the green muscle car raced off down the street. She calmly pushed the button to close the garage door, her face a mask of anger.

Sinclair drove straight to River's apartment, parking out front and running up the twelve flights of stairs to get to her floor. She opened the door with the key River had given her and walked inside. The radio was on in the bedroom. She dropped her car keys on the kitchen table, took off her jacket and put it one of the chairs. She went into the bedroom, and kicked off her boots even as River looked up from the book she was reading.

"Hey, babe. I thought…" River began as Sinclair crawled onto the bed and lay down with her face against River's stomach, her arms around her waist. "What happened?" River asked, moving her hands to Sinclair's hair, gently removing the tie that held it up so she could run her fingers through it soothingly.

Sinclair shook her head, sighing at the feel of River's hands. River continued to slide her fingers through Sinclair's hair. It didn't appear that she was hurt, but she hadn't expected to see her for a couple more days. Sinclair had told her she'd be out of town for a few days, as she was frequently. She'd been surprised to see her walk into the bedroom. She'd been even more surprised by Sinclair's action, although little by little Sinclair was softening in her presence. Slowly but surely, the tough exterior of Sinclair Ryerson was falling away, revealing an intelligent, sweet, thoughtful woman that River became more and more attached to every time they were together.

After a while, Sinclair sat up, resting her head against River's shoulder and wrapping her arm behind her back, holding her tight, her hand curled around a handful of her shirt. River was rubbing her shoulder with one hand, smoothing over her arm with the other, sometimes reaching up to stroke Sinclair's hair back from her face affectionately, often accompanied by a kiss to her forehead.

"Can you talk to me, Sin?" River asked softly.

Sinclair shook her head slowly.

"Okay," River said. She knew that probably meant that whatever was going on was related to Sinclair's business dealings, and Sinclair never told her about that kind of thing.

After about an hour, Sinclair moved her head, nuzzling River's neck affectionately, kissing her ear, her neck, and then her jaw.

"I was going to make some tomato soup, since it's so cold today," River said.

"Sounds really good," Sinclair said.

"Good."

"My grandmother used to make tomato soup," Sinclair said, smiling fondly.

"She did?"

"Yeah, I've missed that. I know my grandfather has her recipe somewhere... I wonder if I could find it."

"So your grandmother has passed?" River asked gently.

"Yeah, we lost her about five years ago."

"But your grandfather is still living?"

"Yeah, he's a feisty guy," Sinclair said. "He's not going anywhere without a fight."

River smiled. "It sounds like you are really fond of him."

"Oh, I love him more than anyone. He and my grandmother raised me when my parents died."

"Your parents died?"

"Yeah, plane crash when I was twelve. My grandparents, my dad's parents, took me in."

"It's good that you had them," River said sadly. "But I'm sorry that you went through that. Losing parents has got to be difficult."

"Where do your parents live?" Sinclair asked.

"Here in Los Angeles, Culver City."

"Do your siblings live here?" Sinclair asked.

"Yep, all of them. And you're an only child, right?"

"Yep," Sinclair said, smiling.

"Kind of lonely," River said sadly.

Sinclair shrugged, resting her head against River's shoulder again. River leaned down to kiss her lips softly. Sinclair reached up, touching River's cheek, then slid her hand back to her neck to bring her closer to kiss her in return. It quickly turned heated—it had been a few days since they'd been together, and that was all it took to make River crave Sinclair. Minutes later they were making love and driving the neighbors crazy with their screaming as they made each other come over and over again.

Afterward they lay together sideways on the bed, Sinclair propped up on her elbow, looking down at River, who lay on her back, her hand to her chest as she breathed heavily, still smiling dreamily.

"I missed you," Sinclair said, her green eyes searching River's.

River smiled softly. "I missed you too, babe."

Sinclair lowered her head, kissing River on the shoulder.

"Mmm…" River murmured. "I love when you do that." She reached up to touch Sinclair's face affectionately.

"Do what?" Sinclair asked, sliding her hand over River's stomach, grasping her waist to pull her closer.

"Pretty much everything."

Sinclair lowered herself to the bed, nuzzling River's shoulder, then her neck, as she settled herself against and around River's body. River happily snuggled into Sinclair's embrace, feeling sated and happy.

Sinclair thought to herself, *Why can't I just stay right here?*

It was a thought she'd have over and over again during the next four months. She found herself spending more and more time in Watts in River's apartment, and less time at the house in Bel Air even when Tracey was home.

Catalina noticed that she saw less and less of Sinclair and began to worry. She texted her on her regular phone, sending a message through her service; it was three days before Sinclair answered. Catalina asked her to come have coffee; again it took three days for Sinclair to answer.

"So, did one of us piss you off?" Catalina asked as they sat outside, in the far corner of the coffee place.

Sinclair lit a cigarette, her eyes reflecting surprise at the question as she shook her head.

"Okay, then where have you been?" Catalina asked.

Sinclair shrugged. "I've been UC for a while," she said casually.

Catalina narrowed her eyes. "Is your case getting ready to close?"

"No. Well, I'm getting where I need to be, but not quite there yet."

Catalina nodded. "Is there another reason you're looking to escape?"

Catalina and the group had met Tracey on two occasions, and

at neither time did any of them like her; nor did Tracey like the group. She felt that far too many of them were too "blue collar" for her taste. She'd also said that she thought the group was far too "occupationally incestuous." Sinclair had needed to get clarification on that one. Tracey had explained that she felt far too many of them worked for the same place, and therefore had lost all objectivity in their profession.

"They're cops, Tracey," Sinclair had said. "Cops are always like family."

Tracey had simply looked back at her like she couldn't fathom what she was saying. Sinclair had quickly given up.

"I…" Sinclair began, aware that she'd broken a cardinal rule in UC work, which was to not mix up your personal life with the cover. She was embarrassed to admit that to Catalina.

"What is it?" Catalina asked, reaching out to put her hand over Sinclair's.

Sinclair shook her head, looking away, her eyes reflecting the conflict inside her head.

"Sin," Catalina began softly. "It's obvious something's wrong, and if you're hitting the cover this hard, then it's trouble at home. So what's going on?"

Sinclair blew her breath out, shaking her head again. "It's not just something going on at home—it's something going on in my cover too."

"Okay," Catalina said, nodding and waiting for the rest.

"There's a woman that I met," Sinclair began. Catalina immediately closed her eyes in consternation, but she didn't interrupt. "I was completely drawn into her," Sinclair continued, shaking her head. "I know it was stupid, and I know that it's not something I should have ever started. But I did, and now I just want to be there, and not here…"

"Jesus, Sin," Catalina said gravely. "Please tell me she doesn't have anything to do with the case."

"She doesn't. I met her through the case, but she's not really connected to anyone from it—just a very minor player, and in a very minor way."

"Okay, but she's still connected and could still completely blow your cover," Catalina pointed out.

"I know."

"You haven't told her who you really are, have you?"

"No, but I want to so often," Sinclair said, shaking her head.

"Don't," Catalina said. "It could get you killed, Sinclair. You never know how that's going to go, and you can't take that chance."

Sinclair grimaced, nodding. She knew it was what she needed to hear; it just didn't make it any easier to hear.

"Are things with Tracey that bad?" Catalina asked.

"They aren't good—they're never good anymore," Sinclair said. "And things with River are so… easy."

Catalina nodded, drawing in a deep breath. She was worried now for her friend. She'd done undercover work long enough to know that as soon as things became personal for you, you lost all objectivity. There'd been so many times during the course of a case when Catalina would encounter someone that she wanted to rescue from that life, or someone that she wanted to be honest with about who she was. It was difficult to pretend to be the exact thing you were fighting against. In your head you knew you were doing it to take down the people that sold or manufactured the drugs you pretended to sell. In your heart you began to feel more and more soiled by the people you had to be around all the time. An undercover cop needed that safe haven of a life to come back to that was warm and inviting. Tracey wasn't providing that life for Sinclair, and it made Catalina hate the woman even more than she already did.

To Catalina, Tracey was a self-absorbed, stuck-up, stone-cold bitch, and the poorest example of a butch she'd ever met in the gay community. It had been obvious from moment one in Tracey's presence that she held no value in what cops did, and therefore what the woman she claimed to love did. That alone would have been bad enough, but the fact that she was consistently denigrating Sinclair also irritated Catalina. She'd overheard Tracey telling her not to drink so much, commenting about her language and complaining about her smoking. Tracey didn't seem to care that Sinclair needed to blow off steam after pretending to be someone she wasn't for days at a time. Tracey didn't get it—it was as simple as that, and what was worse, Tracey didn't care if she didn't get it.

"You know you can't stay there," Catalina said.

"I know," Sinclair said. It was something that nagged at the back of her head all of the time.

"And you really need to do something about Tracey," Catalina said. "Maybe take a break, some time off from the job, and just deal with your relationship."

"When?" Sinclair asked cynically. "She's never home."

"So make her be home. If your marriage means anything to her, she'll get that she needs to be there. It's fight for it or let it go, Sin."

Sinclair blew her breath out, nodding her understanding. She was trying so desperately to straddle her two worlds, and it was getting more and more dangerous.

A week later she found out how much of her perspective she'd lost. She got to River's apartment before River got home from work one day. She took a shower and put on sweat pants and a T-shirt, even pulling on her sweat jacket since it was cold in the apartment. River rarely used the heater because she said it cost too much. Sinclair turned on the iHome she'd bought for River for her birthday the previous month, including a new iPod for her as well.

Half an hour later she was lying on the bed, her arm up over her eyes, relaxing and listening to music. The song "How" by Lisa Loeb came on; the first lines hit home. "Didn't come this far for you to make this hard for me." The song went on to talk about the person wanting to know why she felt the way she did, and equating it to asking how a person's heart beat, or why they breathed. Sinclair felt like that was how it was with River; how could she not want to be there? She did it because she had to; it was a biological imperative. She was so caught up in the song she didn't sense the other presence in the room.

When the track ended, she heard someone clear their throat. She jumped, sitting up, her hair, loose from the tie she usually kept it in, flowing around her shoulders. Eddie stood staring at her, almost gaping.

"What the fuck!" she exclaimed in shock and near terror.

"Sorry," Eddie said as he saw her hand move away from the gun resting on the nightstand. "The door was kinda open, and I knocked…"

Sinclair blew her breath out, shaking her head. She realized then that her hair was loose. She reached immediately for the tie on the nightstand, making a show of pulling up her hair to cover the fact that her heart was pounding almost out of her chest.

"So what's up?" she asked, her tone all business.

"Got some shit I need handled," Eddie said, catching that he'd surprised her in her personal space.

"Okay, what are we talking here?" Sinclair asked impatiently.

"Distribution problems." Eddie said, his look pointed.

"And what do you want me to do about them?"

"Take care of it," Eddie said. "Permanently."

Sinclair's chin went up as she got the message; he was ordering a hit. *Damnit, Eddie.* Now she knew she'd have to take him down too at the end of all this. She nodded, her look calculating.

"So who are we talking about?" she asked, all business.

"The same two fuck-ups we dealt with before."

"Guess they didn't get the message the first time, huh?"

"Nope, still skimming, and it's pissing Tony off."

"I'll take care of it," Sinclair said, nodding. "But this is adding to my rap—I expect to get paid."

"Tony knows that."

"Okay," Sinclair said. "Now get outta here before River gets home."

Eddie grinned. "So you and the hot redhead, huh?"

"Yeah, so get the fuck out before she gets here—need some play before business…"

"Nice!" Eddie said, his eyes reflecting his excitement.

"Out!" Sinclair said as she got up off the bed, her eyes menacing.

"Okay, okay," Eddie said, holding up his hands in surrender.

He left a minute later, and Sinclair sat back down on the bed, blowing her breath out. She knew she'd just about completely blown her cover. Things were getting dangerous; Catalina was right. She was losing perspective, and she needed to get her shit together before she managed to get herself killed.

"Was that Eddie?" River asked, walking into the room and seeing Sinclair sitting on the bed.

"Yeah," Sinclair said in as normal a voice as she could manage.

"What's going on, babe?" River asked. She could see that Sinclair was shaken, and it worried her.

Sinclair shook her head. "He just surprised me, is all. I guess I left the front door ajar and he walked in."

"He did?"

"He said he knocked," Sinclair said as River sat down on the bed next to her. "It's just not a good thing to be surprised in my line of work—surprise can sometimes come in the form of a bullet to the head, ya know?"

River winced at the visual, and Sinclair grimaced immediately.

"Sorry, babe," she said.

She knew she shouldn't have said that to River, and she moved to hug her, closing her eyes. She was definitely losing perspective here. That had been the cop talking, not the drug dealer. Holding River close for an extra few moments, Sinclair kissed the side of her head then leaned back.

"I'm gonna be outta town for a few days, babe. I got some business to handle," she said.

"Okay," River said, searching Sinclair's eyes. "Are you okay?"

"Yeah," Sinclair said. "I just need to deal with some issues."

River nodded. She knew Sinclair was purposely not telling her more than she needed to know. Suddenly River felt the urge to tell Sinclair that she loved her, but she knew that it was likely to scare the woman off. They were a casual thing, even if Sinclair spent so much time in River's apartment; she practically lived there. Sinclair had also bought a few things for the place, including a good set of cookware and a better TV—River had had a lousy old tube one. She'd also bought a couch, because she wanted to be able to sit with River when they watched the new TV. Sinclair had said it was a package deal—River had laughed at the phrase, thanking Sinclair for hours on end that day.

Now, looking up at her, River felt the strongest desire to declare her love, but she could see that Sinclair was already mentally distancing herself. River knew that "dealing with issues" meant doing serious business, and it worried her. Every time Sinclair disappeared or "went out of town," she worried that she would never come back, that she'd get arrested or worse. It had occurred to River a couple of times to talk to Sinclair about getting out of the business, but she knew that was dangerous on a number of levels. Part of her knew this relationship was doomed, but she just couldn't bring herself to end it.

Sinclair left the apartment half an hour later. She got into her

Challenger and drove toward the city. She kept her eyes on her surroundings, making sure she wasn't being followed, as she always did when she left Watts behind to head either home or to the office. She parked six blocks from the LAPD offices and walked in, constantly checking to make sure no one was paying attention to what she was doing. In the office she made arrangements for the two men that Eddie had been referring to to "disappear."

She knew things were getting dangerous. Eddie knowing that she was seeing River heavily enough to locate her at River's apartment worried her no end. She'd done her best to keep the two separate, afraid that if things got messy they'd use River against her. What scared her the most was that it would work. She knew if she was smart, she'd go with what she had at that moment and do her best to make the case and get out of Watts for good. She'd been seriously considering Cat's offer of a job, because she knew it would give her a fresh start. She knew that part of her reluctance was that she'd have to leave River behind. It was the last thing she wanted to do.

Sinclair spent the next two days trying to get her head around the idea that she needed to break things off with River. That she needed to distance herself from her and finish making her case against Tony. She couldn't see any other way to keep River out of danger and make her case at the same time. In the meantime, she needed to deal with things with Tracey. Cat's words rang in her head; she knew she needed to either fight for her marriage or let it go. With that in mind, she called Tracey. She was sitting out on the back deck of the Bel Air house, smoking and drinking a beer for fortification.

Tracey answered her phone on the fourth ring. "Hello?"

"Trace, it's me."

"I'm on my way to a meeting. What do you need?"

It grated on Sinclair's nerves that Tracey always made it sound like Sinclair was forever needing something and forever bothering her while she was doing her important work.

"When are you coming home next?" Sinclair asked.

"Why?" Tracey said, instantly defensive.

"Because I think it's time we had a serious discussion about the state of our marriage, that's why," Sinclair said, doing her best to keep her ire at bay.

Tracey was silent for a long moment. "Hopefully that means you've made a career decision."

"Why would it have to mean that?"

"Because what you do for a living is untenable," Tracey said condescendingly.

"To who?" Sinclair asked sharply.

"It's changing you, Clair, and not for the better."

"In your opinion."

Tracey didn't answer.

"So that's it?" Sinclair asked, her tone reflecting her shock. "I need to give up my career to make you happy?"

"You need to give up the undercover work, at the very least."

Sinclair breathed out, hating the sudden tears in her eyes.

"Did you ever love me?" she asked, so much hurt in her voice that it made her ache inside to hear it. "Or did you just love the idea of the perfect little doll on your arm?"

"Don't get all dramatic."

"No, wouldn't want that," Sinclair said, suddenly feeling sick. "I'm gonna go."

"Clair…"

"Bye," Sinclair said, hanging up as soon as the word was out of her mouth.

She set her phone down slowly and stood up. Walking inside, she went to the liquor cabinet—yet another antique—and opened the door. She pulled out a bottle of whiskey and picked up a glass. She went back outside and quietly got drunk for the next two hours, eventually passing out in their bed, then woke up and did it again. Apparently at some point she'd drunk-texted Catalina, because the next thing she knew, Catalina was walking out onto her back deck, followed by Cody, Lyric, Quinn, Jet, and Remington.

"Thought we'd come drink with ya," Quinn said, holding up a bottle.

Catalina leaned down to hug Sinclair. "This sucks," she said. "I'm sorry."

Sinclair swallowed against the lump in her throat, nodding, unable to formulate a reply. She couldn't believe these people had come to commiserate with her. After a couple of hours, more of the group arrived: Jovina, Natalia, Raine, Kashena, Sebastian, and even Jericho Tehrani. By the time the afternoon had turned into evening, the entire group was at the house. Many of them ended up in the main living room, watching soccer. Pizzas were ordered; others brought food in.

"This is a helluva place," Catalina said to Sinclair at one point.

"I inherited it," Sinclair said, glancing around at the house.

"Nice. So she won't get it if you two split?"

"Don't know," Sinclair said. "Inherited it before we got together, but we took possession together and remodeled it together. So I really don't know."

"Sierra!" Catalina yelled across the room, beckoning the one lawyer in the group.

Sierra came over, grinning at Cat, who was obviously a bit drunk.

"So, we've got a legal question," Cat said. "If Sin here inherited this house before she got together with bitch face—that's what we're calling her now, isn't it?" she clarified with Quinn, who stood behind them.

"Yeah," Quinn said, laughing.

"But then they took possession and like remodeled together, does that mean bitch face gets half?"

Sierra grinned again, rolling her eyes at the name. Then she looked at Sinclair.

"Did you take out a loan to do the remodels?" she asked.

"No, I used some of the inheritance money for that."

"So there was no loan, nothing she helped pay back?"

"Right."

Sierra smiled. "Then it's your house."

"Ha!" Catalina said happily.

Sinclair laughed, finding that it was more amusing watching her friends get drunk than it was for her to be drunk herself.

Later, she was sitting out on the back veranda, looking down at the lights of Los Angeles—a number of people had checked on her. Cody walked over, sitting down in the chair next to hers.

"So Cat tells me you've had kind of an undercover other life going on," she said gently.

Sinclair glanced at her sharply, surprised that Catalina had told her that.

Cody held up her hands in a defensive gesture. "She told me because she knew that being undercover is how I met and fell in love with Kenna." She nodded to her fiancée, who was on the other side of the pool, talking to Lyric and Savanna.

"Seriously?" Sinclair asked.

"Yep," Cody said. "Now, I wasn't involved the way you are, but I was also investigating her."

Sinclair's eyes widened. "Whoa."

"Yeah." Cody grinned. "And it worked out okay, so… don't dismiss the possibility that if this thing with your girl is worthy, it might not be totally lost."

Sinclair looked back at Cody for a long minute, nodding slowly. She was still fairly sure she was screwed where River was concerned, but it did make her feel a bit better that she wasn't the only one that had fallen for someone while undercover. And at least she hadn't fallen for someone she was investigating; that would have been so much worse.

"So how'd you get out of that one?" she asked.

"I cleared her as a suspect first," Cody said. "And then told her everything and let her ask as many questions as she wanted, and answered them no matter how hard they were."

Sinclair nodded, thinking about how many strikes she had against her, not the least of which was that she was married. Then there was the fact that by now she'd been lying to the woman for nearly nine months.

Tracey walked into the quiet house. Glancing around, she immediately saw evidence that there'd been a party. She noted that there were a number of liquor bottles in the recycling can as well. It annoyed her no end that apparently those friends of Sinclair's had converged on their home and predictably not cleaned up after themselves. In the master bedroom, she found Sinclair lying on the bed; it was obvious she'd passed out there, because she was fully dressed, even still wearing her boots. Tracey made a point of dropping her suitcase loudly on the hardwood floor. Sinclair jumped and then cringed visibly, holding her head.

"Be a little louder, will ya?" she growled.

"I can, if you'd like," Tracey said mildly.

"Oh, I'm sure."

Tracey had no patience for over-imbibing, and less patience for hangovers. "You asked me to come home—I'm here," she said magnanimously.

"Lucky me," Sinclair muttered as she climbed off the bed and went into the bathroom.

It was ten minutes before she emerged, not looking any less hungover. She moved past Tracey and headed for the kitchen to make strong coffee. Tracey followed her, her impatience obvious. Sinclair pointedly ignored her while watching the coffee stream from the machine.

"Are you going to talk?" Tracey asked.

"There's nothing to talk about, Tracey," Sinclair said evenly. "You've made it clear that I'm not what you want anymore. So we can just get a divorce and be done with it."

"Just like that?"

"Yeah, just like that. Just like I didn't realize there was a clause in our wedding contract that stated I wasn't allowed to grow up or change at all."

"I don't think you understand," Tracey began, but Sinclair heard her phone ringing and marched past her to the bedroom to pick it up. It was the nursing home. She answered immediately.

Minutes later she was striding out of the bedroom, keys in hand as she put on her jacket.

"Where are you going?" Tracey asked.

"My grandfather is sick. I'm going over to the home to see what's going on."

"But I came home so we could talk," Tracey said, outraged.

"Well, he takes precedent over you any day of the week, so get over it," Sinclair said, before slamming out into the garage and climbing into her Mercedes.

Three hours later, she was reeling. Her grandfather was very ill, and was being moved to the ICU at Cedars Sinai. She went to the hospital and waited to hear what was going on. Her grandfather had pneumonia and a bacterial infection. Fortunately, Finley Taylor was on duty and had heard the name Christensen; she had come out to see if it had anything to do with Sinclair. She was able to go and assess Abe's condition and then came back to talk to her.

"Okay, we're going to take care of him. He's really sick—the nursing home was right about that—but he's in good hands now. We've got him on oxygen right now, and we're giving him antibiotics for the infection."

Sinclair grimaced. "Can I see him?"

"Of course," Finley said. "Come on."

Sinclair spent the next three days at her grandfather's bedside, barely sleeping and not eating at all. Finley came in on the third day, putting a sandwich and a bottle of water in her hands and telling her to eat.

"Do it, or I'll put you in a bed next to him and feed you through a tube," she said, narrowing her eyes at the other woman.

Sinclair nodded tiredly.

Finley checked Abe's pulse, blood pressure, and oxygen levels.

"He's doing really good," she said.

Sinclair nodded as she chewed. "Any idea why the home didn't catch this sooner?" she asked. "Before it got this bad?"

Finley blew her breath out. She knew Sinclair was having a rough time—she'd been at the house in Bel Air with the rest of the group a few nights before—and she wasn't sure how much more she wanted to heap on the woman.

"Well," she began tentatively, "the fact is that nursing homes aren't really designed for people with fragile health. They're spread too thin."

Sinclair nodded. "So you're saying he needs someone with him all the time?"

"I'm saying it would be better if there was someone to keep a better eye on him specifically."

"So, like a full-time nurse…"

"I think he needs that, yes."

Sinclair nodded, her expression pensive. Finley left the room a little while later. Sinclair thought about what she'd said for the next few hours. She'd received a text from Tracey earlier that day, saying she was headed for Hong Kong. Sinclair hadn't even answered her. Tracey hadn't asked how Abe was doing; Sinclair was beyond caring at that point. She knew Tracey couldn't care less about her grandfather, and it was just one more thing in Sinclair's book.

By that evening, she knew what she needed to do.

Chapter 4

Track Day, as Talon was calling it, dawned with Talon picking Parker up in her blue Lamborghini Aventador SV Roadster. Parker simply shook her head as Talon drove up to her house in Long Beach.

"Probably just scared the crap out of the neighbors," Parker told Talon as she walked up to the porch.

This time Talon was dressed in much more butch-looking clothes—faded jeans, a Harley Davidson tank top with a Harley Davidson jacket over it, and black cowboy boots. She wore some makeup, but not much. She still looked hot, and Parker had to remind herself that she was more than twenty years older than the girl.

"This place is cool," Talon said, looking around the wide porch of the Craftsman-style house.

Parker grinned. "Yeah, I have a thing for old houses."

"Can I see inside?"

"Sure," Parker said, opening the front door and gesturing for Talon to precede her.

The first thing Parker did was to give a whistle, and Bandit came running into the foyer.

"Sitze!" Parker ordered. Bandit's butt hit the floor, his tongue hanging out as he looked at Talon.

Talon smiled, glancing at Parker. "Is it okay to approach him?"

"Just not directly," Parker said. "Turn slightly to the side and put your hand out, so he can check you out first."

Talon did as she was told, and Bandit sniffed her hand, then nosed under it to get her to pet him.

"Hi, boy," Talon said, going down to one knee to rub his face. "Where was he hit? I don't want to hurt him."

"Left lower half of his hind leg—you're fine," Parker said, appreciating that Talon had thought of that.

Once Talon had given Bandit a good rub down, Parker had him sit again.

"Voraus," Parker said, and Bandit turned and left the room.

"What language is that?" Talon asked.

"German," Parker said. "It's what he was trained using. Guess I'll be going English with the next one."

"Kai trains in English?"

"Yeah, unless the dog has previous training in German. Bandit was born and trained in Germany."

"Oh," Talon said, nodding.

Parker gave her a tour of the home, and Talon found herself once again completely surprised by her.

"I had no idea you could do all this stuff," she said.

"What stuff?" Parker asked.

"You know, like refinishing wood, and building and all that..."

Parker grinned. "I'm a card-carrying butch."

"Oh, yeah—see? My card keeps getting lost in the mail," Talon said, her green eyes sparkling.

"'Cause ya wear makeup."

"Damnit!" Talon said, laughing.

"It's okay—it looks good, even when you're trying to look butch."

"Oh my God, Parker, I think that was some kind of compliment. Be still my fragile little heart…"

"Fragile, my ass," Parker muttered.

Talon gasped dramatically, holding her hands to her heart. "You just cussed too."

"Where do you think the phrase 'cussing like a sailor' came from, babe?" Parker said, her blue eyes sparkling.

"Oh, yeah, true," Talon said, then gave Parker a pointed look. "Were you just behaving yourself previously?"

"Probably," Parker said, grinning. "But if you're gonna drag me out to meet your friends…"

"Excuse me, they're not just my friends—they're your boss's friends too."

"Yeah, but I'd already gotten away with telling her no."

"I don't like that word," Talon said, narrowing her eyes.

"I've gotten that," Parker said wryly.

"You can't spend your entire life hiding out. You need to get out and socialize!"

"Who says?" Parker asked, even as she followed Talon out the front door, turning to lock it.

"Me."

Parker chuckled, shaking her head as she followed Talon to her car. Once inside, Parker looked around; it was definitely a nice car. She didn't even want to imagine how much it had cost, but Talon was a movie star, so it wasn't too surprising that the kid could afford it. She still marveled at the thought that she was hanging out with a movie star on her day off, and a very young one at that—it boggled the mind. The kid had so much energy; Parker wasn't sure where she got it all. She didn't remember being that energetic even when she was that young. Talon seemed like she was powered by a motor all the time; it was a bit exhausting.

"I could have driven over to Fontana myself, you know," Parker said as Talon started the two-hour drive back to the track.

"This is your day—I wanted you to be able to relax."

"Not likely," Parker said as Talon took the on-ramp to the freeway at high speed, making Parker reach out to grab the dashboard. "For God's sake, Talon, we're not on the race track yet. Slow the hell down."

Talon heard the cop talking and grinned, gunning the engine and causing the car to leap forward.

"I'm kind of regretting accepting this invitation at the moment," Parker said.

"Will you please, for all that is holy, relax!"

"If you could keep it under a hundred, I might be able to."

Talon glanced over at Parker, her green eyes sparkling with excitement. Parker shook her head, seeing that the girl absolutely got off on taking chances.

"Fine, but if you get me killed, I'm gonna come back and haunt you," she said, crossing her arms in front of her chest.

"Sounds fun," Talon said, laughing as she gunned it again.

By the time they reached Fontana—in record time—Parker had actually gotten to the point of enjoying herself. She could feel the power of the car, and she liked the feeling. At one point, while talking about something and making her case, Talon reached over and put her hand on Parker's thigh at the same time that she took a curve at breakneck speed. Parker was surprised to feel her body respond to the girl's touch. Her mouth went a bit dry, and something inside her hoped desperately for Talon's hand to move up. Parker clamped down on the thought; this girl was a kid, half her age! What was wrong with her?

As Talon took the exit to get to the race track, Parker's phone rang. Talon immediately reached over, turning off her radio so Parker could hear. Once again, she could only hear Parker's half of the conversation, but she could tell it was Chelle again, and that she was yelling.

"What?" Parker asked, looking shocked. "Wait, wait, Chelle. What the hell are you… No, I didn't say that. If she doesn't want her… I—Chelle, will you listen? I didn't say a word about her. If Kim doesn't want her around the baby, you need to respect that. Why? Is it that permanent that she needs to be around our granddaughter right now?" Once again a flash of pain crossed Parker's face.

Talon narrowed her eyes, not liking that Chelle was stirring up pain in Parker. She reached over, putting her hand on Parker's leg, sympathy in her eyes. Parker glanced at her, nodding in appreciation for the show of support.

"No, Chelle, you can't make Kim do anything, and why would you put her through that right now? She needs less stress, not more,"

Parker said. "No, I don't think you should. Because Kim has said she doesn't want you to—when are you going to start listening to what our daughter says?" She narrowed her eyes, shaking her head. "Well, no, I'm not going to talk to her, so if that's what you're looking for, it's not going to happen."

Apparently that wasn't what Chelle wanted to hear, because Parker had to hold the phone away from her ear suddenly, and Talon could hear Chelle screaming. Parker sighed, shaking her head, waiting for Chelle's voice to come down a couple of decibels. When she put her ear to the phone again, she found that Chelle had hung up.

"Bye," Parker muttered as she put her phone back in her pocket.

"You have a daughter?" Talon asked immediately.

"Yeah," Parker said.

"And a granddaughter?"

Parker chuckled. "Yeah, she's only about two months old."

"And your daughter's name is Kim?" Talon asked, not sure if she was ever going to catch up when it came to Parker.

Parker nodded. "Yes."

"How old is Kim?"

"She's only nineteen," Parker said. "Just moved out on her own about eight months ago. Right after she found out she was pregnant."

"Who had her?" Talon asked.

"Chelle had her, but we did it all together. She's been mine since the second she was born."

"And Chelle's doing what now?"

"Trying to get Kim to let the new girlfriend see the baby," Parker said, a haunted look in her eyes.

"Wait, your ex is seeing someone already? How long has it been since you two broke up?"

"The divorce isn't even final yet, but that wouldn't matter—this girl is who she left me for."

"Oh my God, Parker," Talon said, ever shocked by what all Parker was handling.

Parker shrugged. "It is what it is."

Talon chewed on the inside of her cheek, not sure how Parker could be so easygoing about everything. She knew that if it were her, she'd be throwing shit and cussing up a storm. Parker was just handling it and doing her job and being a nice person at the same time. It was amazing.

They arrived at the track a couple of minutes later. Talon could see that many of the group were there already, because of the cars in the lot. The upper echelon of DOJ had turned out in force, since Kashena's Mercedes was there, as was Cat's blue 370Z, and Sebastian's black Hummer, as were Rayden's Jaguar and Jericho's red Challenger Hellcat. Quinn Kavanaugh, Kai Temple, Remington LaRoché, and Memphis Lassiter had shown up as well. Even Legend Azaria and her wife, Riley, had come out to support Talon and her friend.

As they walked up to the group, Talon was happy to see that her newest friends were as supportive of new people as they were of each other. She'd been learning a lot about the group over the last few months. Most specifically Jet Mathews, whose story she was learning because she was about to play her in a movie. In getting to know all of them, Talon had felt like she was part of something for a change, and something that had substance. She'd heard about all the things they'd done as a group, like the time most of them had gone to rescue Memphis. Another instance was when they'd all worked together during an earthquake to help the citizens of Los Angeles and West Hollywood affected by the quake. They were forever showing up for their friends, most recently for another new comer, Sinclair Christensen. Talon hadn't been there, because she'd had a previous engagement, but she'd thought it was great that they all turned up to help out their friends and their community.

Introductions were made all around, and then the challenges began.

"The one to watch for is little Memphis here," Quinn told Parker. "She beat all of our collective arses in Vegas a year or so ago."

Parker grinned, looking at Memphis. The girl was very slight, but did have an intensity about her. As the racing started, the group crowded around the track.

"I hear you drive a Cougar?" Quinn said to Parker.

"Yeah, a '68."

"Nice," Quinn said. "I have a '70 Charger and a '69 Mach."

"Two? Nice…" Parker said, grinning. "I'd like to see them sometime."

"Happily. Legend drives a '70 'Cuda, Remi has a GTO, Jet has a '67 Fastback, and of course the Falco girls all have Ferraris."

"You're definitely into your cars here," Parker said, nodding in approval.

"Oh yeah."

Later, Parker met Dakota and Jazmine, who'd arrived late. She'd heard that Dakota was a contractor.

"I should talk to you about some work I need done at my house," Parker said.

"What do you need done?" Dakota asked, interested immediately.

"I got some issues with my subfloor in my living room. Do you work on older homes?" Parker knew it was a more specialized area and that not all contractors had that kind of experience.

"How old are we talking?" Dakota asked, with an odd light in her eyes suddenly.

"'Bout 1918 or so."

Jazmine started to grin, glancing at Dakota, who widened her eyes.

"Please tell me it's a Craftsman," Dakota said.

"It is…" Parker said, giving her a sidelong glance.

Dakota nodded, smiling widely. "I have been dying to work on another one. I fully restored the one we live in," she said, gesturing to Jazmine.

"Oh, then I'm in the right place," Parker said. "We need to talk."

"Happily," Dakota said.

"Are you planning on driving today?" Talon asked Parker as she walked over, smiling at Jazmine and Dakota.

"Yeah," Parker said. "We were just talking Craftsmans."

"Oh God, house talk!" Talon said, shaking her head. "Come on." She took Parker's arm and led her over to the cars. "Pick!" she said, gesturing to them.

There were a number of exotic cars to choose from, including a race car.

"Well, you did tell me I was supposed to drive a race car…" Parker said, grinning.

Talon laughed. "Then pick the race car."

"Okay. You riding with me, or racing me?"

"Guess," Talon said, widening her eyes.

"Too easy."

Talon chose a Ferrari Berlinetta.

"That's a lot of horsepower," Parker said.

"Watch it…" Talon said, narrowing her eyes at her.

In the end, Talon, Parker, Jet, and Skyler raced. Talon beat everyone hands down, pulling it out easily. As she climbed out of the low-slung Ferrari, she made a face at Parker, who only shook her head, grinning. Talon was happy to note that she wasn't a sore loser at all.

As the next group got ready to go, Kai walked over to Parker.

"I understand we're going to be working together here soon," she said.

Parker nodded, looking a little somber.

"Your dog is okay, right?" Kai asked. She knew that would be the most important thing for Parker.

"Yeah, he's good," Parker said. "He's healing well."

"Good," Kai said. "They retired him?"

"Yeah. But I've got him."

"Yeah, I have the first dog I ever worked with too. He's getting up there, but still one of my best friends."

"What breed?"

"Afghan Shepherd. Kind of got him over in the Middle East."

Parker nodded. "What branch?"

"Marines."

"I was Navy."

Kai grinned. "Yeah, we called you guys when we needed a ride."

"Yeah, I'd give ya a ride—on the bow of my submarine," Parker countered smoothly.

Kai laughed. She already liked the woman.

"So how'd you end up with your dog?" Parker asked.

"He was part of a pack trained to attack American soldiers," Kai said.

"I'd heard about that kind of thing. So what happened?"

"I couldn't let my guys shoot them," Kai said, shaking her head. "The enemy, yeah, but not the dogs. They were just doing what they were trained to do."

Parker nodded. "Yeah, they'd never understand."

"Exactly!" Kai said, glad that someone else understood the logic. "Anyway, he was the pack leader, and I just basically got down at his level and talked him down—not before he managed to give me a pretty good love bite," she added, grinning. "Which is why his name is Digger."

Parker laughed. "I get that. I've had a few experiences like that."

"How long have you been working with the dogs?"

"About twelve years now."

"Jesus, how long have you been PD?"

"Seventeen years."

"Wow." Kai grinned. "You might be teaching me a thing or two."

"Maybe," Parker said, winking at her.

"Alright, what's going on over here?" Finley asked as she joined them.

"Talking dogs," Kai said.

"Yeah, that's new," Finley said, rolling her eyes as she smiled.

"Parker, this is Finley, my fiancée," Kai said, sliding her hand around Finley's waist and pulling her closer.

"Please don't tell me you were a Marine too," Parker said humorously.

"Oh God no." Finley grinned. "I'd die."

"Fin's a doctor," Kai said.

"I see," Parker said. "Handy."

Kai laughed. "Sometimes."

Later, Talon walked over with Jet Mathews.

"Parker, this is Jet. I didn't know if you two had ever met. Jet works for DOJ too."

"LA IMPACT, part of COID," Jet said, holding her hand out.

Parker nodded, taking Jet's hand and shaking it. "Good to meet you."

"You too," Jet said, her light green eyes sparkling.

"Jet is who I'm playing in the movie I'm working on," Talon said.

"Really?" Parker asked, surprised.

"Can't seem to talk Legend out of it," Jet said, rolling her eyes.

"You have to meet Jet's wife," Talon said. "She went off with Cody somewhere," she added, glancing around.

"Wife?" Parker asked, thinking Jet looked like a major player.

"Oh yeah," Jet said, grinning.

"Fadiyah is Iraqi," Talon said. "She's from Raqqa. Did I say that right, Jet?"

"Yes, perfect," Jet said. Talon was a quick study.

"Jet went back to Raqqa to rescue Fadiyah from ISIS-controlled territory," Talon said, excited.

"Wow," Parker said, her eyes widening.

"Yeah…" Jet said, rolling her eyes. "It's what's got Legend all het up to make this movie."

"You sound thrilled," Parker said.

"Oh, trust me—if Fadi wasn't all for it, I'd have said not just no, but hell no."

"So your wife wants to make your story a movie?" Parker said.

"Because she thinks Jet's a hero and wants everyone to know," Skyler said, coming up from the side.

"Shut it, Sky," Jet said.

"Bite me, Jet," Skyler replied, grinning.

"Sky and Sebastian actually went with her," Talon said, nodding toward Sebastian, who stood not too far away.

"What did I do?" Sebastian asked, having heard his name.

"Went with me to Iraq," Jet said.

"If I'd known there'd be a movie about it, Jetfire, I probably would have opted out."

Parker laughed. "Not interested in being famous?"

"Not in the slightest."

"But what you guys did was amazing," the petite blonde standing with Sebastian said.

"This is my wife, Ashley," Sebastian said, touching her fondly on the shoulder.

"Hi," Ashley said, smiling at Parker.

"Hi," Parker replied, smiling in return. "So how did you three manage to go to Iraq, in ISIS-controlled territory no less?"

"We got help from Midnight Chevalier," Jet said. "And from Jericho," she added, nodding toward the DLE director.

Parker looked sufficiently impressed. "The AG and the director?"

"Yep," Jet said. "I was an Army reserve, and Baz and Sky were both previous Army—Baz was a Ranger."

Parker nodded. "Well, it apparently worked."

A woman with long dark hair walked up to Jet then, and Jet put her arm around her, glancing over at Parker.

"Parker, this is my wife, Fadiyah. Fadi, this is Parker. She's part of DOJ."

Fadiyah turned toward Parker, her silver-gray eyes sparkling in the sunlight. "It is very nice to meet you," she said, extending her hand.

"You too," Parker said, nodding to her and thinking Jet had had good reason to go back and rescue this girl. "So how did you two meet?"

"That's the other really cool part of the story," Talon said, grinning as she looked at Jet.

"Fadiyah saved my life," Jet said. "I was hit by an IED, and Fadi was the one that nursed me back to health."

"Holy shit," Parker said, shaking her head. "I think if I was Legend Azaria I'd want to make a movie out of your life too."

"Thanks, that's helpful," Jet said, looking like she meant anything but.

Parker laughed. "Sorry."

"S'okay, Sky's probably next," Jet said, grinning.

"I don't think so," Skyler said, shaking her head.

"You don't think what?" Devin asked as she walked up.

"I don't think I'm letting Legend make a movie about us," Skyler said, smiling at her. "Parker, have you met Devin? This is my wife."

"Nope," Parker said. "Nice to meet you."

Devin smiled. "You too."

Later, in Talon's car on the way home, Parker's phone rang. Talon glanced at the display, since the phone was in her cup holder, and saw the name Kim. Parker surprised her by hitting the speaker on the phone.

"Hey, babe, what's up?"

"Hi, Mom," Kim said. "Have you talked to her?"

Parker grinned. "Yeah, she called me earlier."

"Can you believe her!" Kim exclaimed. "I don't want that chick near me or my kid."

Parker looked circumspect. "Well, that's up to you, babe."

"Do you think I should let her see my daughter?" Kim asked, clearly surprised.

"I didn't say that," Parker said cautiously. "I said it's up to you."

"I don't like her."

"Okay," Parker said, smiling slightly at the loyalty Kim was showing. It made her feel good.

"And I really can't believe what Mom's doing to you—I really can't."

"Okay, but that's between her and I. It has nothing to do with how much we both love you. You know that, right?"

Kim blew her breath out audibly. "I know, but still… She wasn't even there for you when you got hurt, and I was so busy with Ginny…"

"I'm fine, honey, nothing to worry about."

"Right, you say that, but I know you're not, and Mom knows that too."

"Hey, don't worry about me, okay?" Parker said. "You have enough to worry about. Just relax—I don't want your blood pressure

105

going up again. You just worry about yourself and my granddaughter, okay?"

"When are you coming by?" Kim asked. "I haven't seen you in days…"

"Well, I'm not even in my own car right now, so it's not going to be tonight," Parker said, but then saw Talon signaling her. "Hold on a minute, honey. What?" she whispered to Talon.

"I can take you over there."

"You don't need to do that," Parker said. Talon had already done so much for her today.

Talon smiled. "I'd love to."

"Mom, who's that?" Kim asked.

"She's someone I'm working with," Parker said. "And someone you might actually want to meet." She grinned. "Since you're a major fan of hers."

Talon looked over at Parker, surprised, then nodded vehemently.

"Who?" Kim asked.

"Talon Valois," Parker said.

"Are you shitting me?"

Parker grinned. "No, I'm not, and watch your mouth."

"I'm an adult now, Mom—I can cuss. And please, please, please, Ms. Valois, bring my mom over here to see me."

"I'd be happy to," Talon said.

"Awesome!"

"We'll be there in about an hour… or less, depending on how

low Talon flies in this thing," Parker said.

They got to Kim's apartment an hour later, but only because Parker had asked Talon to stop so she could buy some things for her, including diapers and formula.

"The baby was premature, because Kim had preeclampsia," Parker had explained. "They've only been out of the hospital for two weeks. And she's on her own—the boyfriend took off the minute he heard she was pregnant."

"That sucks," Talon had said.

"Tell me about it. I've been trying to convince her to move home so I could at least help out, but she's being stubborn."

They got out of the car; Talon helped carry the bags from shopping. She found that this side of Parker was quite intriguing. She hadn't pictured the woman as a mother, let alone a grandparent.

Walking up to the apartment, Talon could see Parker looking around at the dingy corridor and surrounding apartments. She could tell she didn't like where her daughter was living; it was no wonder she didn't want her to stay here.

Kim opened the door and hugged her mother. The girl had blond hair and pretty blue eyes. She was very petite, and didn't even look like she'd just had a baby.

"Kim, this is Talon Valois," Parker said, grinning.

"It's really great to meet you," Kim said, smiling and extending her hand. "I absolutely love your movies, and you were fantastic in *For the Telling*."

"Thank you," Talon said, taking Kim's hand in hers and covering it with her other hand. "Your poor mother's been stuck with me, planning a fundraiser."

"On a Saturday?" Kim asked.

"Oh, not today," Parker said as they walked into the apartment and set the bags down. "Today Talon was taking pity on me, and she planned a race day."

"A race day?" Kim asked, glancing over at a baby's bassinet as she sat down.

"Can I?" Parker asked, looking at Kim.

Kim smiled. "Of course, Mom."

Talon watched as Parker reached into the bassinet to pick the tiny baby up. It was obvious from the look on her face that she was absolutely enchanted. When the baby fussed a little bit, Parker talked to her softly, and the baby calmed immediately.

"Mom's got the touch with her," Kim said to Talon.

"Which is why you should move home with me," Parker said.

"Mom, I told you, I need to be an adult right now. And you have enough upheaval in your life."

Parker sat down in a chair, smiling at the baby. "Did it ever occur to you that I might be a little bit lonely and you two would be company?"

"It occurred to me that you're still recovering from being wounded, and you need sleep and peace to do that," Kim said, sounding very adult in that moment.

Parker rolled her eyes. "Just like your mother."

"Which one?" Kim asked jokingly.

"The other one," Parker said, grinning.

"I don't think I want to be compared to her right now," Kim said, disgust in her eyes.

"Kimmy…"

"No, Mom—no, you're not going to defend her to me," Kim said, holding up her hand. "She left you for some woman that's like three years older than me. She's lost her fucking mind."

Talon glanced over at Parker and saw the flash of pain cross her features. She did her best to disguise it by looking down at the baby, but Talon had seen it enough times to recognize it. She reached over, touching Kim on the hand and shaking her head slightly. Kim looked at Talon in surprise, but nodded her understanding.

"How's Bandit?" Kim asked. Talon nodded in approval.

"He's good," Parker said, looking relieved at the change in topic. "Getting stronger every day."

"That's good. He's probably living the good life at the house, huh?"

Parker smiled. "Yeah, he's definitely on a permanent vacation."

A little while later the baby started to fuss.

"She needs a bottle," Kim said.

"I'll get it," Parker said, standing up and looking at Talon. "Want to hold her?"

"Me?" Talon asked, looking afraid suddenly.

"You've never held a baby before?" Parker asked.

Talon shook her head.

"Well, always a first time," Parker said, winking at Kim, who grinned.

She carefully handed the baby to Talon. "Support her head on your arm there... right... perfect..."

She left the room, heading toward the kitchen.

Talon looked over at Kim. "She's really sensitive about your mom and her right now."

"I was hoping she was getting better about it, but I could just kill my other mother."

"Well, take it easy on Parker. She's really going through it right now."

Kim nodded, her expression curious. "So you two are working together?"

"Yeah, on a fundraiser for the women and children's shelter."

"But you did a race day for her?"

"Yeah, she needed to blow off some steam, plus it gave her a chance to meet some friends of mine that would be a good support system for her."

"Why?"

"Well, a lot of them are DOJ too, like her, and they've all been through a lot of shit, so they understand what she's going through."

Kim nodded, seeming pleased by Talon's answer. Parker came back into the room then, with the bottle.

"Want to try feeding her?" Parker asked Talon, raising an eyebrow.

"Oh hell no," Talon said, looking terrified.

Parker chuckled, taking the baby back and holding her as she gave her the bottle. Talon watched, fascinated.

Later, as they left Kim's apartment, Parker hugged her daughter.

"You call me whenever you need a break, okay?" Parker said. "I have everything at the house that I'd need to babysit, and you know I'd love to do it."

"I know, Mom," Kim said. "And I will, I promise."

"Please also think about moving back in? I can fix the fourth bedroom up for Ginny, and you could be in your old room, right next door."

"I'll think about it, okay?"

"Okay," Parker said. "I love you."

"I love you too," Kim said, hugging her mother again.

"It was nice to meet you," Talon said, smiling. "Your daughter is beautiful."

"Thank you," Kim said. "It was really cool to meet you too. Keep an eye on my mom for me, will ya?"

"I can probably do that."

"I'm standing right here..." Parker said, her tone low.

Kim and Talon laughed.

On the way back to Parker's house, Talon looked over at her. "She really loves you."

Parker grinned. "She should—I raised her."

"I know, but you know how some people love their parents, but they don't really like them much?"

"Yeah."

"Well, she not only loves you, but she really likes you too. And I think that says a lot about you."

"What does it say?" Parker asked with a quizzical look.

"It says you must have been an awesome parent."

Parker glanced over at the other woman, surprised, but she just nodded.

Talon drove back to her condo that night thinking that Parker Gaines had so much more to her than she'd realized. And Parker had been through hell in her personal life lately, and Talon was determined to help her loosen up and live a bit again. Somehow, Parker had suddenly become her project. *God help the poor woman*, Talon thought, grinning as she gunned the engine of the Lamborghini.

Chelle waited for Parker impatiently. It had been two days since she'd traveled down to Los Angeles for a job interview, and Chelle was dying to know how it had gone. As Parker walked out of the passenger area, Chelle knew instantly that she'd gotten the job. Giving a scream of joy, she ran over and threw herself into her arms.

"You got it?"

"I got it," Parker said, laughing as she hugged Chelle to her.

"Holy crap! We're moving to Los Angeles!" Chelle said, both excited and scared at the same time.

Parker had discharged from the Navy a month before. They had the house on the market, and Parker getting a job with LAPD was the final piece. They'd both wanted to get back down to California. Since the market had taken an upswing in Washington lately, they were pretty sure they were going to get multiple offers on the house and make good money off it. Money they planned to sink into something in Los Angeles. Parker had already been looking while she was down there and had hired a real estate agent to help them. Everything was falling into place nicely.

A month later they'd sold the house, made a small fortune off it, and found another Craftsman in Long Beach, California. It was a bit of a drive for Parker, but it was worth it. The place needed work, but they were both so used to working on a house that it wouldn't be new to them at all. It was perfect!

Chapter 5

River was worried sick about Sinclair; she hadn't heard from her in a week. It had taken everything she had not to ask her relatives to check for her arrest or to start calling hospitals to see if someone like Sinclair had been brought in or, God forbid, murdered...

She was at work when she got a text.

SINCLAIR: Need to talk to you, can you get off work?

RIVER: Of course, are you okay?

SINCLAIR: Yes, I'm okay. I'll be out front in half an hour.

RIVER: I'll be there.

River was waiting outside the clinic when Sinclair pulled up in the Challenger.

"Get in," Sinclair said, leaning over.

River did, seeing that Sinclair looked like she hadn't slept for days. She immediately reached over, hugging her, so relieved that she was okay that she couldn't help herself. Sinclair hugged her back, holding her for an extra moment or two, in case she never got to do so again. Then she sat back, put the car into gear, and started to drive.

"What's going on?" River asked. She knew she wasn't supposed to ask questions, but was too worried about Sinclair's absence and subsequent text to be cautious at that point.

Sinclair didn't answer for a few moments, blowing her breath out, shaking her head.

"I don't even know…" she began, but her voice trailed off as she shook her head again.

"What is it?" River asked, worried that she was about to be arrested, or that she had to leave the country, or any number of horrible things.

Sinclair glanced over at River and saw the worried look in her eyes. She blew her pent-up breath out again, and when they reached a stop light, Sinclair unlocked the glove box and pulled out the badge she'd stopped at the house to get before coming to meet River. She handed it to her as the light changed, and started driving again as River stared at the badge in her hand.

"What is this?" River asked, suddenly terrified that Sinclair had killed a police officer and was getting ready to run.

"That's mine," Sinclair said.

"Your… what?" River asked, thinking she meant a souvenir or something.

"It's my badge, River. I'm a cop."

River's mouth fell open. "You're a…"

"Cop—undercover narcotics for LAPD."

River blinked a few times, absentmindedly tracing the design on the badge with her fingers. "And you've been undercover… with me?"

"Well," Sinclair said hesitantly, "I've been undercover and I've been with you. The two are not mutually exclusive."

"So you're not really Sinclair Ryerson," River said, her tone slightly sharper.

"Christensen," Sinclair said. "My last name is Christensen."

"And your first name?"

"Is really Sinclair."

River nodded. "Am I a suspect?"

"No," Sinclair said. "You never were, really."

"Really? I never was *really*?"

"You never were," Sinclair said. "But I needed to assess how well you knew Eddie or any of his dealings."

River stared back at her, her eyes reflecting hurt and anger. "So that's what you were doing when we were fucking? You were assessing me?"

Sinclair winced at River's tone. "No, that's not…" she began, trailing off as she accelerated past another car and took the next freeway exit.

She drove to a semi-private area where she could park, then turned to River.

"When I met you," she said, her look direct, "I wanted you instantly. But I had to make sure you weren't connected to the case I'm working. That's why I asked you about how well you knew Eddie. That's all."

"But you're working a case against Eddie?"

Sinclair stared back at her for a long moment, then nodded slowly.

Cat had looked at her like she was insane.

116

"You're going to tell her everything?" she asked, then started shaking her head. "You can't. You'll destroy your cover and you'll probably get yourself killed!"

"She's not part of that, Cat—I know that," Sinclair said.

"But you don't know if she'd run back and tell them, and you won't know that till they put a bullet in your head. No, you can't do it."

"I have to," Sinclair said beseechingly. "I have to, Cat."

"Sinclair…" Cat said, shaking her head sadly. "You'll get yourself killed."

"I have to try."

"Should you be telling me any of this?" River asked, suddenly recognizing the danger this posed to Sinclair if she was really an undercover cop.

"No," Sinclair said. "No, and believe me, I could get fired for doing it."

"Then why are you doing it?" River asked suspiciously.

Sinclair blew her breath out audibly. "Because I need your help."

"I'm not a cop, and I don't know anything about what Eddie does," River said, holding her hands up defensively.

"It's not about the case."

"Then what?"

"It's my grandfather. He's been really sick," Sinclair said. "I've been with him at Cedars for the last three days."

"And not getting any sleep, I see," River said. She was still angry, but Sinclair took heart in the fact that she'd noticed and still cared enough to comment on it.

Sinclair smiled slightly. "I was worried."

River nodded, seeing that Sinclair was still worried. "So what do you need my help with?"

Sinclair looked back at her, aware that right now everything seemed so simple....

"I need to bring him home with me," she said. "And then I need a nurse to be with him, someone I trust."

River stared at her for a long moment. "But your apartment..."

"Isn't my apartment—it's a department issue."

"So you have enough room for your grandfather?"

Sinclair chuckled softly. "Yes."

"So are you asking me to come be your grandfather's nurse?"

Sinclair pressed her lips together. "Yes, and I really wish that was everything I had to tell you, but it's not."

River sensed from Sinclair's tension and tone that she was about to be blindsided.

Sinclair took a deep breath, blowing it out slowly. "I'm married."

"What?" River asked, feeling all the blood leave her head.

Sinclair winced, but nodded. "I'm married."

River breathed out heavily, closing her eyes for a long moment. "Please don't tell me you're married to a man..."

Sinclair gave a soft laugh, shaking her head. "No, I didn't lie about being a lesbian."

River looked slightly relieved, but then the truth of it came back to bear.

"You're married," she said.

Sinclair nodded, her expression pensive.

River nodded too, her lips tightening, her eyes narrowing.

"I'm really having to resist the urge to hit you right now," she said. "And you should know I'm only resisting that because I'm still holding your badge and I know better than to assault a peace officer."

Sinclair pressed her lips together. Reaching over, she took her badge out of River's hands and tossed it into the back seat.

"Do it," she said, her look pained, her hands on her legs relaxed.

River searched Sinclair's eyes, seeing the anguish there and not understanding it, but also not able to strike her. She shook her head sadly, turning to gaze out the window.

"I need to think about this…" she said distantly.

Sinclair drew in a deep breath, nodding. "Okay. I'll drive you back."

The drive back to River's apartment was achieved in stony silence. Sinclair was sure she could hear her entire world crashing down around her, but refused to say any more. She couldn't beg; it was just too hard. She sincerely hoped River would at least be willing to help with her grandfather, but she had no idea if that was even possible. At the apartment, River climbed out without even looking at her. Sinclair waited until she was inside before putting the car in gear and driving away.

River walked into her apartment and looked around. She saw all of the things that Sinclair had bought for her, the couch where they'd lain watching soccer matches and movies. She went into her bedroom, and when she looked at the bed, she thought she felt her heart being wrenched out of her chest. Lying down, she could smell Sinclair on the pillow she always slept on—she threw it across the room with a scream. Then the tears started, and the anger came next. She screamed and yelled and threw things. It was the worst night of her life.

Sinclair's night was worse. She soared between depression and out-and-out rage. She lay in her bed and stared up at the ceiling, feeling like part of her life had already been ripped away. She'd checked on her grandfather again, and seen that he was doing better. She'd talked to Finley about what all she would need to do to make him comfortable. She tried to ignore the ache in her heart that kept threatening to overwhelm her.

It had been two days since she'd told River about who she was and had asked for her help. She hadn't heard a word from her. Sinclair steeled her heart and returned to work to get more paperwork handled to make the transfer to DOJ. She'd also met with Catalina and Rayden to discuss joining LA IMPACT that same day. Because of the meeting, she was dressed in indigo jeans, a burgundy button-up shirt, dark brown boots with a two-inch heel, and a dark brown leather jacket that matched the boots. She also wore makeup, and her hair was pulled back at the top, the rest hanging loose.

She looked very different, and it was the first thing River noticed when Sinclair stepped out of the building, lighting a cigarette and immediately taking a deep draw before she continued toward the parking garage.

"Sinclair?" she said, stepping out from behind a column.

Sinclair stopped, her expression reflecting her surprise.

"I…" Sinclair stammered. "Hi."

"Hi."

"How?" Sinclair asked, gesturing to the building.

"LAPD," River said, shrugging. "It wasn't too hard."

"How did you know I was here?"

River just shook her head. "You look like a girl," she said, smiling.

Sinclair chuckled softly. "Sometimes."

"Is this what you normally look like?" River asked, taking in the makeup, the hair, the heels…

"Sometimes," Sinclair repeated. "Other times more butch."

River nodded, trying to assimilate what she was seeing.

"I was headed to my car," Sinclair said, gesturing toward the parking garage.

"Okay," River said, and indicated for Sinclair to lead the way.

Sinclair smoked her cigarette, glancing over at River as she walked.

"How's your grandfather?" River asked.

Sinclair smiled. "He's doing better. Finley's keeping an eye on him for me."

"Finley?"

"One of my friends—she's a doctor at Cedars."

"Oh."

They got to the parking garage and Sinclair led her up the stairs to where her car was parked, crossing the lot to the sleek blue Mercedes. She stopped to open the trunk.

"Your car?" River asked, her eyes wide.

"Yeah."

"So the Challenger is…"

"Mine too, just not what I drive unless I'm undercover."

River nodded, still looking shocked.

Sinclair put her gear bag into the trunk, closed it, then turned to lean on the car. "So…" she said, looking askance at River.

"Are you headed to see your grandfather?"

Sinclair stared back at her for a long moment, then nodded. "Yeah, that was my plan. Why?"

River canted her head. "Can I come meet him?" she asked softly.

Sinclair blinked a couple of times, but then nodded as she smiled. She opened the passenger door for River. River climbed inside, looking around at the luxurious interior. It didn't fit with the Sinclair she thought she'd known. Neither did the woman climbing in on the driver's side. She looked completely different.

As Sinclair started the car and backed out of the parking space, River glanced over at her.

"I have a small confession to make," she said.

"What's that?"

"I checked you out."

Sinclair glanced at her, raising an eyebrow. "And you did that how?"

"Well, I never told you, but I have connections with law enforcement."

"What kind of connections?"

"Well, connections with the DA's office, and with the LA sheriff's office too."

"I see," Sinclair said, thinking she'd been lucky her cover hadn't been compromised before she'd admitted to River who she was.

"So," River said, "my brother, who is a detective for the sheriff's office, told me you were absolutely insane to tell me who you are and especially when you then took me home without even asking me not to say anything to anyone. That it could have gotten you killed so easily…"

Sinclair's eyes flickered as she nodded.

"Why would you do that?" River asked.

Sinclair didn't answer; she simply tightened her hands on the steering wheel.

"What else did you find out about me?" she asked after a few long moments.

River narrowed her eyes slightly, noting that Sinclair hadn't answered her question; she wasn't sure what that meant.

"I found out that you're very good at what you do," she said. "That you've closed more cases than anyone in your division."

Again Sinclair's eyes flickered, her lips twitching slightly.

"How long have you been married?" River asked.

Sinclair let out a snort. "You didn't get ahold of my personnel file too?"

River widened her eyes at her tone, but she shook her head. "That's confidential."

Sinclair made a noise in the back of her throat. "Well, at least something is."

"What does that mean?"

"If you wanted to know something, you could have asked."

River narrowed her eyes slightly. "I wasn't sure if you'd tell me the truth."

Sinclair glanced over at her, then inclined her head, her mouth set in a hard line.

They were both silent for a long couple of minutes.

"Five years," Sinclair said.

River nodded, swallowing convulsively. Part of her still wanted to scream and hit things, including Sinclair for lying to her, for letting her fall for her and then snatching it all away with two simple words: "I'm married." It still rang in her head all the time. The woman she was in love with was married! And not to some man, but to another woman!

They were both quiet then. When they reached Cedars, Sinclair parked the car and turned to River.

"Look, I'm sorry," she said evenly. "I just... This isn't easy for me either. I couldn't tell you who I was, and by definition couldn't tell you that I was married. I know I fucked this up—I know that and I'm sorry, I really am, but..." She shook her head, looking stricken as she turned away. When she looked back at River, there was a naked plea in her eyes that made River hold her breath. "I can't lose him, and I can't trust just anyone. I... I need you, River. And I'm sorry—I am. Please…" she said, her voice so soft and so desperate, River knew she'd do anything for her.

"Let me meet him," River said, just as softly.

Sinclair nodded and got out of the car. River got out too and they walked into the hospital together. They went up to the appropriate floor and Sinclair signed them in, then led River down to a room. Walking inside, Sinclair smiled brightly at the older gentleman sitting in the bed.

"Hey, Dad," Sinclair said, hugging her grandfather and kissing him on the cheek.

"There's my beauty!" Abe said, hugging her and smiling.

"Dad, I want you to meet someone. This is River. River, this is my grandfather, Abraham Christensen."

River stepped forward, extending her hand to Abe. He took it, bringing it up to his lips and kissing the back of her fingers.

"I'll bet you do that with all the girls," River said, smiling.

"Only the really pretty ones," Abe said, winking mischievously.

"Oh, I recognize that look," River said, glancing over at Sinclair. "I'll bet those blue eyes of yours get you into trouble all the time."

"They get me out of trouble just as often," Abe said, his eyes twinkling. "Let me tell you about the time I got into trouble with one very young but very beautiful actress…"

An hour and three stories later, Sinclair and River left the hospital room. In that time River had found out a few things: that Abe Christensen was very definitely a feisty gentleman, that he adored Sinclair with every fiber of his being, that he didn't like Sinclair's wife, and that Sinclair loved her grandfather more than her own life.

As they waited for the elevator, Sinclair grinned at River.

"He's already got a crush on you," she said.

River laughed. "He does not!"

"Oh yeah, he does," Sinclair said. "My grandmother was a redhead too; he has a thing for beautiful redheads..."

River smiled, recognizing that Sinclair was paying her a compliment and appreciating it. It was just another thing that she loved about this woman. She was always so open in her adoration. It was refreshing to have someone compliment her openly and often.

Back in the car, River turned to Sinclair. "He's the reason you risked your life by telling me who you are," she said. It wasn't a question.

Sinclair nodded. "Yeah."

"I'll do it," River said.

"You will?" Sinclair looked like she wasn't daring to hope that she'd heard what she just had.

"Yes."

The relief that flooded Sinclair's face was almost painful to see.

"Thank you," she said. "You have no idea how much this means."

"I think I do," River said. "I can see it on your face."

Sinclair drew in a breath, nodding.

"So is it possible to see where he's going to be staying?" River asked.

"Of course," Sinclair said, starting the car and pulling out of the parking lot.

They drove for a while, and River wanted to ask questions, but she just couldn't bring herself to do it. Part of her wanted to stay completely ignorant about Sinclair's wife. Abe's references had been things like "Where is she this time?" and "How many locations can you scout in a year?" River wasn't sure what they meant, but she could tell this wasn't a new issue for Abe.

The stereo was playing, and Van Halen's "Why Can't This Be Love" came on. River couldn't help but listen to the first lines and think, *Exactly!* The lyrics spoke of being all wound up inside every time they touched.

God knew that every time she and Sinclair touched she saw her whole world in Sinclair's eyes; she heard it in her voice, and she felt it in every fiber of her being. And no, she'd never felt so much with anyone else, ever. It was crazy. Now to find out that Sinclair wasn't who she had thought, but then to find out that she wasn't the bad parts she'd thought she was either… It was a tangled mess.

"You haven't asked about—" River began, then realized suddenly that there might be a reason for it.

"About what?' Sinclair asked, glancing over as she took a left onto La Cienega Boulevard.

"Never mind," River said, shaking her head.

Sinclair's eyes flickered, but she didn't ask again.

It was another ten minutes, but then they crossed Sunset and Sinclair took a right and started up the curving streets. River started looking around.

"Sin…" she began, trailing off as her eyes widened at the houses they were passing.

"Yeah?" Sinclair asked, her tone matching the grin on her lips.

"Where exactly do you live?"

"In the hills.'

"Which?" River asked, almost breathless.

"Technically, Bel Air."

"Umm," River stammered. "How much do cops make these days?"

Sinclair laughed. "Not that much, trust me."

"But you live in Bel Air," River said. "So are there some small houses up here?"

"I'm sure there are," Sinclair said. "Mine's not one of them though."

"Okay," River said, realizing there was apparently a lot more about Sinclair that she didn't know. "Roughly how big, would you say?"

Sinclair pressed her lips together in thought. "I'd say about seven thousand."

"Feet?" River asked, her voice almost a squeak.

Sinclair grinned. "I don't think they measure in inches, babe."

"Uh-huh," River said, looking shell-shocked.

They came around another curve, and Sinclair reached down into the door to take out a remote. The garage for one of the biggest houses on the block started to open, and River immediately noted the green Challenger sitting inside.

"That one?" she gasped, pointing at the house.

Sinclair chuckled, nodding.

"Oh my God…" River said, shaking her head in disbelief.

It only got worse when Sinclair led her into the house, turning off the alarm. They walked into the front room, and the floor-to-ceiling windows gave River a perfect view of Los Angeles far below.

"This is insane…" she breathed.

"You gonna be okay for a minute?" Sinclair asked. "So I can go put my stuff down?"

River nodded, not taking her eyes off the view. She went closer to the windows, tugging nervously on the sleeves of her hooded sweatshirt. Pulling one of the sleeves down over her hand, she put her hand up to the window, leaning her head against it as she stared out at the view.

When Sinclair came back into the room she was carrying two beers. "I figured you could use this," she said, handing one to River.

"Oh yes," River said, taking the beer gratefully. "How do you not just sit and stare out the window all day?"

Sinclair glanced at the view. "I've lived here for the better part of five years," she said, grinning. "So I've been able to tear myself away finally."

"So you're saying you get used to that?" River asked, gesturing to the view again.

"Wait till you see it at night."

"Ohh…" River said, awed.

"Would you like to see the rest, or are you already done with the part of the tour you need?" Sinclair asked, smiling.

"The rest… please?" River said, enthralled.

The tour of the house did nothing to reduce River's awe. In fact, she was completely enchanted with it, especially the keyhole-shaped marble foyer and the front door, which looked like a castle gate, ten feet high, painted white with black hardware.

Sinclair showed her the lower floor, where she wanted to put Abe. It had its own kitchen area; it was almost a separate apartment with two rooms. They were both large, and River was sure that any medical equipment they needed, if any, would fit easily. She made a few suggestions that Sinclair took note of on her phone. They walked back upstairs.

The last room they went into was the master bedroom, which had a huge picture window. Lying in the bed, you could look out at Los Angeles with no effort at all. The bedroom itself was huge, with a large four-poster bed, hardwood floors, and beautiful antique furniture. Everything was so elegant and rich that River realized she really didn't know Sinclair at all. The bathrooms were all done in beautiful tile and marble with rich, expensive-looking linens. The house was decorated to a tee, and River now found herself feeling like a complete pauper next to Sinclair, whereas before she'd felt more like her equal.

As she glanced around, River saw the wedding picture. It was a large photo, at least two feet by three. Sinclair wore a white wedding gown, looking absolutely breathtaking, next to a woman with short dark hair wearing a gray, pinstriped tailed tuxedo. River couldn't help but stare at this woman. Sinclair's wife. She hadn't pictured Sinclair married to a butch woman, especially not one as butch as this woman looked. She also noted that she appeared older than Sinclair. River glanced back at her and saw that she was looking at the picture as well.

"What's her name?" River asked quietly.

"Tracey."

"She's very..."

"Butch?" Sinclair supplied.

"Yes," River said. "Not what I pictured at all."

Sinclair stared back at her, her lips twitching slightly.

"I'm gonna change," she said. "There's more beer in the fridge if you want another one. I'll be out in a minute."

"Okay," River said, noting that the discussion about Sinclair's wife was over quickly.

When Sinclair emerged from the bedroom ten minutes later, she wore her black yoga pants and a light blue Nike T-shirt, and was pulling on a black jacket. She noted that River had found her way outside to the back veranda and was once again staring out at the view. Sinclair walked up behind her, grinning.

"I guess I know where I'm going to find you a lot, huh?" she said.

River glanced over her shoulder, taking in the outfit. Once again, she was surprised. It was very different from the sweats and baggy T-shirt Sinclair had worn at her apartment. The pants outlined her perfect shape and long, lean legs, the T-shirt was fitted and emphasized the fact that the woman didn't have an ounce of fat on her, and even the jacket showed off her great shape.

Sinclair caught the shake of River's head. "What?" she asked.

"I just..." River started, not sure what to say.

"You just what?" Sinclair asked, curious as to what the woman was thinking at this point.

"I just keep realizing how little I know you," River said, sounding sad.

"You know me better than you think."

River shook her head. "The house, the car, the clothes… Tracey…" she said, her voice softer on the last.

"The house I inherited from my maternal grandmother, along with enough money to keep it maintained and taken care of. The car I bought myself, because I needed something the opposite of my cover. The Challenger belonged to my father. The clothes… They're just clothes. Tracey… Well, that's a whole other story."

"Okay, but when are you going to tell me that story?" River asked, her true concern coming to bear.

Sinclair rolled her eyes. "Well, if we're going to have that conversation, I need Jack," she said, walking into the house. She returned with a bottle of Jack Daniels and two glasses with ice.

River chuckled. At least that was something she recognized; Sinclair always drank Jack Daniels when she'd had a rough day. They sat down on the veranda and Sinclair poured them each a glass. After Sinclair had taken a nice long drink, she sat back, looking at River.

"Ask me anything you want about her."

River took a long drink of her own. "How did you meet her?"

"At an industry party. One that my family throws every year. She was an up-and-coming executive with the studio."

"And you?"

"I was a beat cop at the time. You should also know that I wasn't gay then."

River's eyes widened. "You… you were straight?"

Sinclair grinned. "Yep."

"Wow…" River said, shaking her head. "I never would have believed that."

Sinclair waggled her eyebrows, licking her lips as she grinned.

"So she pursued you?" River asked.

"Yeah," Sinclair said. "She loved how girlie I was."

"Yeah, that wedding picture looked pretty girlie."

"I was extremely girlie then."

"So odd," River said, "because I never thought for a second that you were anything but butch."

"Cover," Sinclair said, widening her eyes.

"And a good one. But you even make a beautiful butch—that's the thing."

Sinclair smiled softly. "That's nice to hear."

"Tracey doesn't think so?"

Sinclair's lips curled into a sardonic grin. "Not quite, no."

River blinked a couple of times, fighting the urge to suggest that Sinclair's wife might need glasses.

"Were you in love with her when you got married?" she asked.

"Yes, I was."

"Do you love her now?"

Sinclair drew in a deep breath, her expression thoughtful, but then shook her head. "Not anymore," she said sadly.

"What changed?"

"Me," Sinclair stated simply.

"What do you mean?"

"I mean, I changed." Sinclair shrugged. "When I got my sergeant's badge, I decided I wanted to go into narcotics, and they talked me into the idea of doing undercover work because there are so few women who do it. I decided to give it a try. When it was time to come up with my cover, I decided to go butch like Tracey, figuring I'd have less issues with guys hitting on me if I was very obviously not into guys."

"Makes sense."

"Yeah, it did to me too, but it didn't sit well with her at all. And then I started discovering that I was more comfortable in some of the clothes and with some of the mannerisms I adopted."

"So you kind of discovered your butch side."

"Exactly," Sinclair said, nodding. "But Tracey didn't like it at all. She married a femme, and that's what she wanted on her arm at parties."

River stared at her, openmouthed. "So she was the only butch allowed in the relationship?"

Sinclair drew her lower lip in, biting it. River had hit the nail right on the head. "You got it."

"Well, that's bullshit!" River said. "Relationships are about give and take, not my way or the highway."

"I don't think Tracey got that memo," Sinclair said, taking another long drink.

"Abe asked where she was 'this time.' What did he mean by that?"

"She travels all the time," Sinclair said. "Weeks at a time."

River was perplexed. "How do you make a marriage work when neither of you are ever around?"

Sinclair laughed. "I think that's probably why it's lasted as long as it has."

"But…" River began, but then shook her head.

"What?"

"You were with me so much."

"Because you were who I wanted to be with," Sinclair said. "I was able to be myself with you."

"Yourself?"

"Okay, closer to myself. You have no idea," Sinclair said, shaking her head.

"No, I don't," River said. "Tell me."

"God, babe…" Sinclair said, searching River's eyes. "I was exactly who I wanted to be when I was with you."

"In what way?"

"Emotionally, romantically, sexually…"

"Sexually?" River asked. "Are you different with her than you were with me?"

Sinclair laughed. "Oh, honey, you have no idea at all…" she said, trailing off as she shook her head.

"So that's a yes, you are different with her?"

"Yes, very different."

River bit her lip, wanting to ask how, yet not sure she wanted to know.

Sinclair saw the question in her eyes. Standing in one smooth motion, she slid her hand behind River's neck, pulling her forward to kiss her deeply. River moaned instantly as her body came alive. Putting her hands to Sinclair's shoulders, she grasped at them passionately. Sinclair's other hand reached up between them, cupping River's face, and she groaned as her own passion ignited. A few moments later she pulled back, looking into River's eyes.

"No one makes me feel like that but you," Sinclair said. "No one."

River nodded as Sinclair moved to sit back down. She had to calm her pulse for a moment before she could even think about asking another question.

"So she doesn't make you feel that way?" River had to ask.

"Never."

They were both silent for a while as the sun set and the city lights started to come on below.

"Oh my God..." River breathed. "You weren't kidding about the view at night."

Sinclair smiled. She found it incredibly endearing that River was so enthusiastic about the house and the amazing view. While she had acted blasé, she actually loved it too; she was ever amazed by it. Tracey didn't pay it any attention at all. She took it and the house for granted completely. It irritated Sinclair no end.

The wind came up at that point, making it far too cold to stay outside.

Sinclair stood up, holding her hand out to River to help her up out of her chair.

"Let's go inside," she said softly.

They walked into the house and Sinclair led River back to the master bedroom. She moved to the fireplace just to the side of the large picture window. Kneeling, she lit a match and set it to the wood already in place.

"Caretaker," Sinclair said, gesturing to the fireplace.

"You have a caretaker for the house?" River asked.

"We have to, since both of us are gone so often."

"Oh."

"Can we just sit?" Sinclair asked, indicating the bed.

River nodded. Sinclair kicked off her shoes. River did the same, and they both climbed onto the bed. Sinclair leaned against the pile of pillows, and to her happy surprise, River moved to sit next to her. She felt River shiver slightly; she reached down and picked up the throw at the end of the bed, putting it over her. She then put her arm around her, drawing her closer. River snuggled in, having missed Sinclair so much. She knew things were a mess, and she knew they weren't likely to get easier, but for the moment she was just enjoying the closeness.

Reaching up, she took Sinclair's hand. As she did, she noticed a ring on her finger that she hadn't seen before. It was a simple platinum band, and it was obviously her wedding ring. She rubbed her thumb over it absently, thinking about what Sinclair had told her about Tracey. To her it was unfathomable that Tracey wouldn't find Sinclair attractive even when she was completely butch-looking. She'd been attracted to Sinclair from the first second she'd seen her, and that was long before she'd fallen in love with her. River didn't understand how Tracey could love Sinclair and not love everything

137

about her. It made no sense.

"What's going on in your head?" Sinclair asked softly.

River drew her breath in, blowing it out as she shook her head. "I just don't understand how Tracey can't love all of you," she said, shrugging. "I don't understand that."

Sinclair nodded pensively.

"I just really need to think about all of this. I mean, this part," River said, indicating them.

"I understand."

River glanced back at her. "I'm sorry, it's just… I've never been 'the other woman' before, and I'm not sure it's something I'm comfortable being."

"River, you don't need to explain," Sinclair said. "I honestly figured we were over the minute I told you I was married."

River turned to her in surprise. "You did?"

"Yeah. I just figured that was kind of relationship kryptonite for you."

"Why did you figure that?"

"Well, you didn't want to get involved with me in the first place—so that, on top of this…"

"I didn't want to get involved with a drug dealer, Sin," River said. "Now I know you're not that."

"No, instead I'm an adulterer," Sinclair said, rolling her eyes. "Big upgrade."

"It actually is," River said. "With family in the DA's office and LASO… I was really risking a lot dating you."

Sinclair looked back at her for a long moment, then shook her head. "I'm sorry I put you in that position."

"You didn't know who my family was. I purposely didn't tell you."

Sinclair sighed, nodding.

They were both silent then, each lost in their own thoughts. They fell asleep that way.

The next morning, Sinclair woke to the feeling of River in her arms. They'd gone back to their usual sleeping habits, with River on her side, her back against Sinclair's chest, Sinclair holding her from behind. Without stopping to think, Sinclair lowered her head, kissing River's neck, nuzzling her as she pressed closer from behind.

River woke, feeling Sinclair's warmth surrounding her and her lips against her neck. Reaching back, she slid her hand over Sinclair's thigh, pulling her closer. In moments they were touching and caressing. River turned over, her lips seeking Sinclair's. Neither of them was thinking as the fire between them caught. Clothes were removed and tossed aside, and skin against skin caused them both to gasp. Minutes later they were both crying out in their release.

"Well..." River gasped as she laid her head against Sinclair's chest.

"Mmhmm," Sinclair murmured, breathing heavily as well.

"I just can't resist you," River said, shaking her head mournfully.

"Same here, babe," Sinclair said, kissing River's forehead.

"Are we going to be able to be in the same house without this happening?"

"Not sure," Sinclair said honestly.

"Are we going to try?"

"If you're still willing to work with my grandfather…"

"Of course I am, Sin. I'm not abandoning him," River said, her tone making Sinclair smile.

River had just met Abe once, and she was already devoted to him. It said a lot about who she was, compared to Tracey.

Later that morning, Sinclair discovered yet more endearing things about River. They'd discussed going back over to River's apartment to get some clothes and things for her to stay at the house in Bel Air. Sinclair dressed in faded jeans, a sweatshirt, and combat boots, looking like the butch River was used to again. River watched, fascinated, as Sinclair made coffee in the fancy kitchen, and then as she poured it into a thermal cup to take with her. It was such a contrast—the completely different setting, but the same Sinclair that River was used to seeing.

They got into Sinclair's Challenger and headed to the apartment. On the way, a song came on Sinclair's iPhone that surprised River; it was a Missy Elliott track, a very, very hip-hop rap style, and so completely not what River was used to from Sinclair's music.

"I'm sorry?" River said, looking shocked as she gestured to the stereo.

Sinclair laughed, shaking her head. "That's a Memphis addition."

"A what?"

Sinclair grinned. "Memphis is one of the people I hang out with when I'm not working. She's a DJ and sound person, and she's forever loading new music on people's iPods. She's been known to actually steal Remi's iPod to load new music. She wants to broaden everyone's horizons."

River laughed. "So her way of broadening everyone's horizons is to steal people's iPods and load random music on them?"

"Yeah," Sinclair said. "You have to meet her to understand—she's really cute like that."

River nodded, noting the look on Sinclair's face. "She sounds like a character," she said, smiling. "I'd love to meet her. And Finley too."

"Okay," Sinclair said.

"And she's a doctor?"

"Yeah. She's also the fiancée of my trainer."

"Trainer?" River asked, surprised.

"Well, it's just been over the last several months, since I met Cat and in turn the rest of the group."

"The rest of the group? And who's Cat?"

Sinclair smiled, realizing she had some explaining to do. "Okay, Cat is the one that's going to be my new boss when I transfer to DOJ at the beginning of next week."

"Wait, you're leaving the PD?"

"Yeah. Better pay, better benefits, and Cat will let me cut back my caseload so I can be with Dad more."

"Okay, and Cat is who?"

"Well, like I said, she'll be my boss. She's the Special Agent Supervisor in charge of the Clan Lab group at LA IMPACT for DOJ."

"LA IMPACT?"

"It's a task force. They do drug interdiction, asset development, money-laundering cases, a bunch of stuff at the state level."

"Okay," River said. "So you met Cat through work?"

Sinclair chuckled. "I actually met Cat when she tried to arrest me down in San Diego."

"What!"

Sinclair laughed. "Yeah, she saw me doing my thing, and thought I was a drug dealer and tried to arrest me in the bathroom."

"Oh, wow… How'd that go?"

"Well, we're friends now, right?"

"Okay," River said. "So that's how you met her—but in San Diego?"

"Yeah, she's from down there and was visiting—which was the time I told you my business took me down there, remember?"

"I do remember that now, yeah," River said, realizing how often Sinclair had been honest, but not too honest with her.

"Well, she is part of a group of women that hang out in WeHo, and I've kind of become part of that group. Finley is in it too, along with Kai, the trainer, and a few other very notable women."

"Notable how?" River asked, very curious now.

"Well, there's rock stars, a movie star and director… a retired MMA fighter… the Director of the Division of Law Enforcement for

DOJ, the head of the Criminal Division for the AG's office... sometimes even the AG herself..."

"Wait—Midnight Chevalier?"

"I named all of that, and that's who caught your attention?" Sinclair asked, grinning.

"Well, she's friggin' awesome, so..."

"That she is."

"So—rock stars?"

"Xandy Blue and Wynter Kincade."

"Holy crap! You know them?"

"Well, they're part of the group, so I've hung out with them on occasion. They were at the house not too long ago."

"And a movie star?"

"Riley Taylor—she's actually Finley's mom."

"Oh my God, she's... she's like really, really famous..."

"And her new wife, Legend Azaria," Sinclair said.

"Who is so friggin' hot it's not even funny..."

Sinclair laughed. "Oh, trust me, you need to see some of the butches in this group if you want to see hot. There's Jet, who's over-the-top hot... There's Skyler, there's Dakota and Cody and Lyric—all butch, all hot. Then there's my buddy Quinn, who's a very butch, very Irish kind of hot."

"Wait, is that the one that's Xandy Blue's bodyguard? The one they were calling the White Knight for a while?"

"One and the same," Sinclair said, inclining her head.

"She's your buddy?"

"Soccer—she loves soccer. Her and Jet, actually, and Jovina, Cat's girlfriend."

"So they're all gay?"

"Yep," Sinclair said. "There's more, but you'll just have to meet them all."

"I think I would love that," River said, smiling. "And not just because some of them are famous. You said the Director for the Division of Law Enforcement?"

"Yeah, Jericho Tehrani. And the chief of LA Impact, Rayden Black Wolf."

"You know some pretty important people…"

"Just by luck."

"And they're your friends?"

"Yeah. You'd be amazed at how they come together to support people in their group. I was the lucky beneficiary of it a while back."

"How so?" River asked.

"I was, uh… well, having a rough time with the shit with Tracey, and the fact that I was lying to you… Anyway, I was drinking pretty heavily and actually drunk-texted Cat at some point, because next thing I know, little by little the group showed up to 'drink' with me. They hung out with me, watched soccer, and basically made sure I was okay."

"I like them more and more," River said, smiling.

"*You* will like them."

"Is that your way of saying that Tracey doesn't like them?"

"She doesn't like them, and none of them like her. I believe the term being used the other night for Tracey was 'bitch face,'" Sinclair said, grinning.

"Oh my," River said, widening her eyes. "Now I love them."

"I see…" Sinclair said, happy that River sounded like she was looking forward to meeting the group.

It illustrated a vast difference between River and Tracey. Tracey had been uninterested in meeting the group, and when she finally had she'd spent most of the evening watching them with either a condescending or bored look on her face. It was the reason no one had liked her. The rest of the meetings after that had turned out much the same. No one could understand what someone like Sinclair was doing with someone like Tracey. It made no sense whatsoever. Sinclair was really beginning to see what they meant.

Chapter 6

The night of the party arrived, and both Parker and Talon were working like crazy right up until an hour before the event. Only then did they have time to change. Parker waited by the venue dressing rooms, having promised to escort Talon into the party now that they'd become pretty good friends during their time planning it. She looked extremely dapper in a black tuxedo, with a black shirt and emerald green tie. Talon had insisted on the tie, saying it would match her dress. Parker had shaken her head and agreed to wear whatever Talon asked. She'd given up arguing with the girl; she always got her way, regardless of Parker's protests.

Parker heard the door to the dressing room open, and when she turned around she was fairly sure her heart stopped. Talon looked absolutely amazing in an emerald green Monique Lhuillier gown that molded to her body perfectly and lit her green eyes with sequins and lace. It covered her from collarbone to toes and from shoulder to her fingertips, but was still incredibly sexy. Her black hair was pulled up, with tendrils artfully escaping around her face and neck. Her makeup was perfect, accentuating her eyes and high cheekbones. Parker was speechless.

"I think I need to go change," she said after staring at Talon for a full minute, stunned.

"Why?" Talon asked, smiling brightly, loving the look on Parker's face.

Parker grinned. "Because I look like a slouch now."

"No, you don't," Talon said, walking forward and reaching out to straighten Parker's tie. "You look fantastic," she added, smiling as she brushed back a lock of Parker's hair that had fallen over her forehead.

Cameras captured the moments.

"No," Parker said. "You look... I can't even think of the right word for how good you look." Her smile reached her eyes, making them sparkle.

"Well, then we make a good team."

"I guess we do," Parker said as she turned, offering Talon her arm.

Talon leaned her head on Parker's shoulder for a moment. Cameras clicked away.

The party went off without a hitch. The entire group had shown up for Parker and Talon, lending their support. Midnight Chevalier had also come to give a speech and present the check to the shelter. She'd told everyone how she felt that this night wouldn't have happened nearly as well without the hard work of Talon and Parker. It seemed only appropriate that the two dance after that announcement.

As they did, Parker grinned at Talon. "This turned out well," she said.

"Yeah, it did," Talon said. "Except for one thing..."

"What one thing?" Parker asked, surprised; she thought everything had gone well.

"Well, you're still too far away..." Talon said, stepping closer and pressing herself against Parker as they continued to dance.

"I…" Parker began, then gasped softly as she felt her body once again react to this woman. "Are you trying to see if you can completely blow my composure here?"

"Uh-huh," Talon said as she looked into Parker's eyes, her smile mischievous.

"Why?" Parker asked, searching Talon's eyes.

"Because I want to see if I can."

"Oh, trust me, you can."

Talon nodded. "Good."

"And what do you think's going on there?" Riley asked Legend. They stood with the rest of the group, watching Talon and Parker dance.

Legend grinned. "I think Talon is utilizing her considerable skills."

Riley glanced at her wife quizzically. "Why do you think she's doing that?"

"Because I think she wants Parker, and has all along."

Riley was surprised, but realized that Legend had spent more time with Talon than she had, and it was possible they'd talked about Parker.

"Well, there ya go," Quinn said, seeing Talon move closer to Parker.

"What the…" Xandy muttered.

"Son of a…" Jet said, grinning.

"What is she doing?" Fadiyah asked Jet.

"Making a move."

"Is Talon making a move on Parker?" Skyler asked, leaning past Devin to talk to Jet.

Jet nodded. "I'd say so."

Devin smirked. "She's been hanging around you too much."

"Thanks," Jet said, chuckling.

"Anytime."

Two hours later, in the limo that had been hired to take them home, Parker looked over at Talon.

"You realize that everyone in the group is talking now, right?" she said.

"Uh-huh," Talon said, looking unapologetic.

Parker shook her head. "I don't get what you're doing."

Talon turned to her. "You don't get that I want you?"

Parker stared back at her with her mouth open in surprise. Then she shook her head. "You're screwing with me."

"No, but I'd like to be," Talon said seriously.

Parker opened her mouth to say something, then shook her head.

"Why is that so hard for you to believe?" Talon asked.

Parker's eyes flickered as she gazed back at her, then she shook her head again.

"Talon, I wouldn't know how to handle a woman like you if you came with a full set of instructions."

"It's because of her, isn't it? Because she told you that you were boring and too old."

Parker's lips twitched, the pain flickering over her face as it always did when she thought about Chelle and her betrayal.

"She said that I didn't excite her anymore," she clarified.

"Well, I say she's a fucking idiot, and you excite the hell out of me without even trying."

Parker blinked a couple of times.

Talon took that opportunity to pull the lower half of her dress up and straddle Parker's lap. Without another word she took Parker's face in her hands, leaning down to kiss her, softly at first and then with more pressure.

When Parker's hands moved to her waist, pulling her closer, Talon moaned and began to move her body against Parker's. She loosened Parker's tie and then unbuttoned her shirt, sliding her hands inside to touch skin.

"Wait, wait..." Parker said, breathless, as she shook her head. "The driver, we're—"

"Shh..." Talon said, sliding her hands down to touch Parker's nipples.

"Jesus..." Parker breathed, closing her eyes.

Talon continued to caress her, and felt Parker's hands on her bare thighs. She moaned, pressing her body closer. She unbuttoned and unzipped Parker's pants, slipping her hand inside. Parker jumped and moaned loudly when Talon's fingers slid between her legs, feeling the hot wetness there. Talon spread her legs wider, moving her hips.

"Touch me, Parker... please..."

Parker couldn't ignore that plea and slid her hands up Talons thighs, discovering that she wore nothing under the dress. That only made her hotter as Talon's fingers moved against her. Parker moved her fingers between Talon's thighs, her thumbs spreading her lips as her middle finger touched wetness.

Talon gasped loudly, pressing herself against Parker's finger.

"I want you inside me," she groaned.

That had Parker's pulse tripping as she slid her finger inside Talon, her thumb rubbing at her clit. Talon moved her hips and continued to rub against Parker's pussy. They both came in a rush.

Talon lay against Parker as they both gasped for breath.

"I'd say you know how to handle me just fine," Talon said.

"Jesus..." Parker breathed, laughing. "You are crazy."

Talon grinned against her shoulder. "Oh, sweetie, you haven't seen anything yet."

"God help me."

Talon sat up, looking down at Parker. "Oh, God won't help you," she said, grinning wickedly. "Heaven's afraid of me, and hell's afraid I'll take over..."

"So I'm between heaven and hell here?" Parker asked eagerly.

"Oh yes."

"Well, this should be fun," Parker said, shaking her head.

At Talon's condo, Talon took Parker's hand and got out of the limo.

"We're going inside?" Parker asked.

"Oh, I'm not even close to being done with you yet," Talon said, smiling.

Parker laughed and shook her head, following the woman inside.

Within minutes, Talon had Parker on the couch and they were making love. She then led Parker up the flight of stairs toward the bedroom. Talon took off the dress, and Parker saw that she did indeed have nothing on underneath it. Then Talon started to undress Parker, one piece at a time, all the while kissing her and caressing whatever skin was exposed.

At one point, Parker's butch side asserted itself, and she backed Talon up to the bed, kissing her deeply, her arms around Talon's tiny waist, her hands stroking her skin. She lowered the two of them to the bed, lying over Talon and sliding her hands up over her breasts, making Talon shudder. Then she moved her lips to Talon's neck, and then lower to her breasts, touching, caressing, and grasping with her hands.

Talon put her hands in Parker's hair, guiding her head, moaning at the feel of Parker against her. It was rare that a woman asserted herself with Talon, and it was exciting the hell out of her. Before long, Talon was aching and begging Parker to fuck her, grasping at her and trying to pull Parker down to her. Parker held back, wanting to excite this girl to the point of near insanity before she took her fully.

When Talon was shuddering, her nails cutting into Parker's skin as she tried to pull her down, Parker finally gave in. She slipped her body between Talon's legs and ran her hand down to slide her fingers into Talon as she moved against her. Parker essentially fucked her the way she'd been begging her to. Talon came with a loud scream and continued to move herself against Parker until she came again and again.

After Talon stilled, Parker shifted their bodies, lying on her back with Talon over her. Talon moved down, her body between Parker's legs, her head on her stomach. When she'd caught her breath, she started to kiss Parker's stomach. She felt Parker's hand in her hair immediately. She looked up at the other woman, her green eyes sparkling in almost a predatory way.

"What do you want?" Talon asked, her tone low.

Parker stared back at her, her breathing growing heavy, her lips parted.

"Tell me what you want…" Talon said.

Parker swallowed convulsively, her hand in Talon's hair tightening slightly.

Talon smiled, moving slightly lower and hearing Parker's sharp intake of breath.

"Show me," Talon said, her look pointed.

Parker's hand at her head pressed her lower as she pushed her hips up. It was all Talon needed, and she lowered her head and slid her tongue over Parker. Before long Parker was coming, and Talon thoroughly enjoyed the feel of that power.

After they'd made love half the night, they both lay exhausted in Talon's bed. Talon fell asleep in Parker's arms. Parker shifted slightly, moving away, turning to lie on her back. She reached down to find her phone, which was still in her pants pocket. She texted Kim, who had finally agreed to move home, that she wouldn't be back that evening.

PARKER: Staying at Talon's, will be home later tomorrow (today).

KIM: Hot damn! Go for it Mom!

Parker couldn't help but chuckle. Kim very much liked Talon, and felt like she was making her mother happy, even if they were only friends. It was obvious from Kim's response, however, that she'd hoped for more between the two. Setting her phone on the nightstand, Parker lay back, looking up at the ceiling. She had no idea what she was doing with this kid, but she had to admit to having thoroughly enjoyed herself that evening.

During the night, Talon awoke and realized that Parker no longer held her. She turned over, seeing that she was asleep on her back with her hand on her chest. Normally she didn't really want to be held after sex; she wanted to move away from the person to her own space. "Cuddling" had too weird of a connotation to it in her book, so she didn't normally do it much, if at all, if she could avoid it. However, she'd really liked the feel of being in Parker's arms; something about it had been so good. She didn't take the time to analyze it in the middle of the night, but she did move next to Parker, snuggling under her elbow, until Parker woke enough to move her arm to encircle Talon's shoulders. Talon settled against her, her head in the hollow between Parker's shoulder and neck, and fell asleep again.

In the morning, Talon found that once again Parker had moved away from her and turned over on her side. It was something Talon took note of, because it bothered her in some weird way. She sat up, looking down at Parker. She admired the curve of her neck, and the strong jawline. She brushed the lock of sandy-blond hair off Parker's forehead affectionately. Talon didn't know what it was about Parker that drew her in; maybe it was the fact that her wife of twenty years had been fool enough to let her go for a younger woman, or the fact that she was such a great mother—Talon didn't know for sure. What she did know was that she'd grown very fond of her over the last month.

One day she'd come to Parker's house to talk about some of the plans for the party. She'd texted her ahead of time, and Parker had told her to just come inside when she got there, that the baby was asleep. What Parker hadn't said was that the baby was asleep on her chest. When Talon had walked inside the house, she'd found Parker in the living room, lying on the couch with the baby. It had been such an incredibly sweet moment that Talon had gotten tears in her eyes.

There'd been many more moments like that with the baby, where Parker would be feeding her or holding her, and Ginny would just smile so lovingly at Parker that it was almost painful to see. Talon couldn't understand how Chelle could want to leave someone like Parker when she was obviously so incredible with her granddaughter and in general. Talon developed more and more affection for Parker over that time. It had simply culminated in the occurrence the night before at the party.

Parker stirred, turning over onto her back and opening her eyes. She stared up at the ceiling, confusion in her eyes for a moment, then glanced over at Talon.

"Forget where you were?" Talon asked, grinning.

"Kinda, yeah," Parker said, grinning too.

"I have a question for you."

"Okay," Parker said, sitting up against the headboard, pulling the sheet up with her.

"You kept moving away from me during the night," Talon said, keeping her voice even. "Is there a reason for that?"

Parker looked pensive for a short moment, then grinned. "Yeah," she said. "Because Chelle never wanted me too close—she said I'm like a human heater and it always made her too hot, and not in a good way."

"Oh…" Talon said, nodding. "Okay, yeah, that makes sense." She looked over at Parker. "Am I the first woman you've slept with since the breakup?"

Parker laughed, nodding. "I don't really go in for spreading it around…"

"Kind of a one-woman kinda girl, huh?"

"Kinda, yeah."

Talon nodded, looking pensive suddenly.

"Don't worry," Parker said, putting her hand out. "I don't consider this"—she gestured between them—"anything serious. I get that you're not… well… monogamous."

Talon tilted her head, looking a little shocked. "You get that I'm not monogamous?"

Parker stared back at her, her eyes widening slightly as she half-grinned. "You know you're in the papers all the time, right?"

"Well, yeah," Talon said knowingly. "But that doesn't mean that I sleep with everyone they say I do, you know."

Parker nodded slowly, her eyes wary. "Okay, so how many women do you sleep with regularly?"

Talon opened her mouth, then closed it, her expression contemplative suddenly.

"If you have to think about it…" Parker said, her grin wry.

"Yeah, yeah, I know, okay," Talon said, rolling her eyes. "But maybe you're different."

"And maybe I'm not," Parker said. "What I'm saying is that I get it, okay? I'm not looking for anything heavy at this point, and you… well, you never seem to be looking for anything heavy, so we're good."

Talon stared back at Parker, not sure how she felt about her assuming that she wasn't capable of committing to anyone. In truth, she never had committed to anyone, but hells bells, she was only twenty-three! Did she need to be married with three kids by now? Sheesh!

"But…" Talon stammered then. "Does that mean we're good and I get to still sleep with you, or… does it mean we're good and I've had my one shot at you?" she said, giving Parker a leading look.

Parker grinned. "Let's just see how it goes, okay?"

Talon nodded. "Okay…"

River got her opportunity to meet the group at the Club. It was the night after her first night staying at Sinclair's house. Walking in, River was surprised by popularity of the place. Many exclusively lesbian clubs had failed due to the tendency of lesbians to couple up and stay home. River came to realize later that part of the reason the Club was so popular was the resident DJ, Memphis Lassiter. It was easy to see and hear why. Memphis had a really great flow of music, moving from techno to rock to hip-hop then back to techno. Sinclair pointed Memphis out, and River saw what she meant about the girl; she definitely had an engaging smile, and River could tell that she loved what she was doing. Her wife, Kieran, was in the booth with her, but off to the side—she was adorable as well.

Walking over to the group, Sinclair nodded to everyone as they all looked at River with interest. Cat had told them about River, and who she was to Sinclair, so there wouldn't be any comments or uncomfortable confusions.

"Cat, this is River," Sinclair said. "River, this is Catalina Roché, my soon-to-be boss, and her girlfriend, Jovina Azevedo."

"Hi," River said, smiling at both women. "I understand you tried to arrest Sin the first time you two met," she said to Cat.

"Yeah…" Catalina said, grinning. "She managed to fool me—that's pretty good."

"It's a butch thing—you'd only half understand," Quinn said, winking at Cat as she stepped forward. She extended her hand to River. "I'm Quinn."

"The White Knight," River said, smiling.

"Alright, which of you told her that?" Quinn asked, giving everyone a narrowed look.

"I watch TV with the rest of the world," River said, laughing softly. "And I think you give butches an awesome reputation."

"Oh, I like this one," Quinn said, putting her arm around River's shoulders.

"Easy," Sinclair said, narrowing her eyes at Quinn comically. She winked. "Besides, your girl might have to hurt you…"

"Yes, she might," Xandy said, mock-glaring at her girlfriend, then extended her hand to River with a smile. "I'm Xandy."

River widened her eyes, nodding. "I know—I love your music."

"Thank you," Xandy said, smiling shyly.

"Are you ever going to get used to hearing that?" Quinn asked as she reached out to touch her girlfriend's cheek affectionately.

Xandy laughed. "Probably not."

"Which is just part of why I love you," Quinn said, winking at her.

"River, this is Kai and Finley," Sinclair said.

"The trainer," River said, nodding and smiling at Kai, thinking Sinclair was right about all the handsome butches she knew. "Nice to meet you."

"So you're going to be taking care of Abe?" Finley asked.

"Yes," River said. "I got to meet him yesterday—he's such a character!"

"Isn't he, though?" Finley said, smiling brightly. "I swear he's charmed half my nurses! Kinda like someone else I know..." she added, giving Kai a narrowed look.

"What?" Kai asked, grinning unrepentantly. "It was mostly Jacks... and she wanted me to take you out, so..."

"Yeah, yeah, sure, sure," Finley said, rolling her eyes. "Kai had every nurse in the place, straight or gay, hot for her, when she was in my ER."

"You were in her ER?" River asked, shocked.

"That's how we met," Kai said, grinning and winking at Finley.

"Appendicitis—very nasty, burst long before we got to her," Finley said.

"Wow," River said, her eyes wide. "A lot of people don't survive that."

"I got lucky, and got the best doctor there," Kai said, smiling over at Finley.

"Uh-huh... the one doctor there that already had the hots for you..."

"That's why there's a ring on your finger," Kai said, winking.

"Is that why?" Finley replied, smiling all the while.

River looked at the ring on Finley's left hand and smiled. "That's gorgeous! Not like a boring solitaire kind of ring..."

"Oh, Kai doesn't do anything the boring way," Finley said, smiling warmly. "Come see me tomorrow when you guys come to pick up Abe. I'll give you the rundown, okay?"

River smiled. "Of course."

She was introduced to the rest of the group then, feeling completely overwhelmed. When she met Natalia and Raine, Natalia gave Sinclair a pointed look.

"You're coming to class tomorrow, sí?" she said.

Sinclair grinned. "Yeah, I have a session with Kai, though."

"Ay! No, you can't cheat on me with Kai," Natalia said, smiling widely.

"I'm not," Sinclair said. "I'm just... well... I'm two-timing you both—what can I say?"

"La fulana!" Natalia said, making Sinclair laugh.

"What did she just call you?" River asked, grinning.

"A tramp," Sinclair said. "Natalia is the cardio dance instructor whose class I take when she's not being a complete joda."

Natalia opened her mouth and swatted Sinclair on the ass, making half the group laugh.

"What's a joda?" River asked.

"A pain in the ass," Sinclair said, smiling sweetly at Natalia, who only shook her head, her grin sly.

"So you do a dance class?" River asked as they walked over to the bar.

"Well, Nat's class is a lot harder than just a regular dance class," Sinclair said. "Come with me tomorrow and you can see for yourself."

River smiled. "I just might do that."

Later, Memphis took a break and walked down to the group, smiling and greeting everyone, her blue eyes falling on the newcomer. Remington handed Memphis a beer; she took it, thanking Remington, her eyes still on River.

"Memphis, this is River," Sinclair said, seeing Memphis' curiosity, which she didn't bother to hide.

"Aww," Memphis said, smiling a knowing smile. "I see."

River gave her a quizzical look. "Do I want to know?" she asked, glancing at Sinclair.

Memphis grinned engagingly. "Probably not," she said, widening her blue eyes humorously.

"Alright then," River said, smiling. "I love your stuff," she added, gesturing to the DJ's booth.

"I haven't seen you dance yet," Memphis said, her eyes sparkling.

"I've been meeting people."

"Well, if you're done, come dance with me," Memphis said, putting her hand out.

River looked back at her, surprised, and glanced at Sinclair, who shrugged and nodded toward the dance floor. River noticed that everyone seemed to be watching her at that point. She glanced back at Memphis, who still held her hand out. Shrugging, she nodded and took Memphis' hand, letting her lead her to the dance floor.

The song playing was very much a techno track, called "Go" by MAKJ & M35—in fact, the only words were "It's time to go if you don't dig techno!" River found out quickly that Memphis was a very good dancer, and also very popular; every girl on the floor smiled and either high-fived her or made physical contact with her in some other way. As the song ramped up, however, Memphis slid her hand around River's waist, moving in close and smiling down at her. She found it amazingly fun to dance with this woman.

Suddenly she was part of the crowd on the floor, and adjusted quickly to the way that Memphis moved, moving with her; it was somewhat sexual, but she could tell by the smile on Memphis' face that it was just fun for her. River put her hand to Memphis' shoulder and matched her move for move. Before long Memphis was laughing and nodding approvingly.

Back at the tables, the group was watching the two dance and nodding to each other. They already liked River. Memphis was very particular about who she liked, and her asking River to dance meant she liked the look of her. They could tell from the way Memphis was laughing and moving that she now fully approved of the girl. Memphis was like the group's divining rod for people, because she had the one of the purest spirits in the group—everyone trusted her judgment. If Memphis had reservations about a person, they were suspect to the whole group. Memphis hadn't liked Tracey for a second.

As another song started, Pitbull's "Bad Man," the other girls all went to join Memphis and River on the dance floor. Sinclair watched from the table, seeing how easily River was with everyone; she couldn't help the pull that she felt in her heart. This was how it should have been with Tracey, but it hadn't.

"I like her," Catalina said.

"Me too," Quinn added from her side.

Jet grinned. "I'm in."

"Yeah, well, there's that matter of a wife," Sinclair said, rolling her eyes.

"You could enact the shovel clause," Jet said.

"Huh?"

"That's where you give the word and your friends all show up with a shovel and never speak of the person you buried again," Jericho said, grinning as she winked at Sinclair.

Sinclair laughed at that, shocked that it had come from the Director of the Division of Law Enforcement.

When River finally returned to the table, Sinclair handed her a beer. River took it and, setting it aside, slid her arms around Sinclair's neck, leaning up to kiss her. The group started catcalling immediately. Sinclair grinned against River's lips, sliding her hands around her waist and pulling her closer to deepen the kiss. Memphis, who'd gone back to the DJ booth by this time, got on the mic.

"This is for River and Sinclair," she said, winking at the two.

The song "Right Kind of Wrong" by LeAnn Rimes pumped from the speakers, and Sinclair had to take River out to the dance floor. The bridge very definitely fit how River felt about Sinclair—it really fit them both. Needing each other's touch was definitely very, very true.

The chorus went on to say that even though she shouldn't love Sinclair, it was hard, because God knew Sinclair was so much the right kind of wrong, and River knew she was hooked on the woman in the worst way. She was amazed that somehow Memphis already seemed to see that. Glancing up at the DJ booth, River smiled at her, nodding, and Memphis winked back.

Later in the evening, Sinclair got the signal from Jet and Quinn that they wanted her to go smoke with them.

"The bois want to smoke," she said to River. "You okay?"

"We'll keep an eye on her," Cat said, winking at Sinclair.

Sinclair laughed. "Now I'm worried."

After Sinclair went outside with many of the bois, McKenna moved to sit next to River.

"I heard about how you met Sinclair," she said wryly. "I met Cody much the same way."

"Really?" River said, having met Cody, who was a very young-looking butch. McKenna was a model-level beautiful blonde with blue eyes.

"Oh yeah, but in my case, I was actually a suspect at first."

"Wow…" River said, her eyes wide. "How did you get over that?"

"Well, Cody was right about my husband being a slime, and she basically kept me out of jail by doing a lot of extra legwork to clear me."

"Did you fall for her while she was working the case?"

McKenna grimaced. "That was the worst part."

"What do you mean?"

"I did fall for her while she was working the case—the problem was, she was undercover as a seventeen-year-old girl…" McKenna shook her head. "I thought I was losing my mind, that I was hot for not only a female, but for an underage one as well!"

River blinked a couple of times, completely shocked.

"Okay, see? Now I don't feel as bad!" she said, laughing. "I thought I was crazy, falling for a drug dealer when half my family is law enforcement."

"At least you didn't think you were turning into a pedophile."

"So you weren't even a lesbian when you met Cody?"

"Nope." McKenna shook her head. "But Cody drew me in so completely, I had no choice but to love her," she said, smiling fondly.

"I know that feeling," River said, chagrined.

McKenna's eyes widened. "Are you in love with Sinclair?"

River bit her lip, not sure she wanted to admit to it to one of Sinclair's friends. Finally she just nodded, not looking happy about the thought.

McKenna put her hand sympathetically on River's arm.

"She doesn't love Tracey, you know," she said.

"Tracey is still her wife, though," River said. "And wife trumps affair anytime."

McKenna looked skeptical. "I don't know…"

River appreciated that McKenna was trying to make her feel better, but she was pretty sure she wasn't that important to Sinclair other than in a nursing capacity at this point.

Outside, Sinclair was getting questioned as well.

"So you actually blew your cover to tell this woman who you are?" Lyric asked chidingly.

"I needed her help, Lyric. How else was I going to get it?"

"You couldn't just hire your grandfather a nurse?" Cody asked.

"Not someone I trust. Come on, you know you guys like her."

The bois exchanged a few looks, then started to nod.

"She was a big hit with Memphis," Remington said. "She loves her already."

"Course, she loves Sin too, so…" Kai said, grinning.

Remington laughed. "Yeah, that's true."

"She loves me?" Sinclair asked, surprised. She was fond of Memphis too, but she had no idea the girl really liked her that much.

"She's funny like that," Remington said. "She bonds with people instantly sometimes. Expect your iPod to disappear soon," she added with a grin. "And tell River to watch hers."

Sinclair laughed.

166

Later that night, on the drive home, River looked over at Sinclair and smiled.

"I really had a good time," she said.

Sinclair smiled back. "Good, I'm glad. They really like you."

"They do?" River asked, pleased to hear it. "I think they're all pretty friggin' awesome. Even if I didn't get to talk to everyone tonight."

"Well, not everyone was there either, so... It's a pretty big group."

River nodded. "What was the thing with Memphis?"

"What do you mean?"

"When she asked me to dance, I noticed that everyone was watching me."

Sinclair laughed. "Yeah, Memphis kind of has a keen sense of judgment when it comes to people. If she likes you, then the group likes you."

"Really?"

"Yep."

"And?"

"She loves ya," Sinclair said, smiling.

"Did she like Tracey?" River couldn't help but ask.

"Not for a second."

"Hmm..." River murmured, her expression far too gleeful.

Sinclair glanced at her, and couldn't help but laugh at the look on her face.

When they got to the house, they went into the kitchen.

"So, I think we should try sleeping in our own areas tonight," River said.

Sinclair nodded, doing her best not to look disappointed. She knew River was still trying to figure things out and that she had no right to expect her to rush it on her account.

"We're going to need to get used to it for when Tracey does come home…" River said.

"You don't need to explain, babe. It's okay," Sinclair said.

River bit her lip. Part of her really wanted Sinclair to argue with her, but she knew she was trying to respect her feelings and wishes on this, and she loved that about her.

Two hours later, River stood in the doorway to the master bedroom. She saw that Sinclair was lying on her back, staring up at the ceiling.

"You've got that view, and you're looking at the ceiling," she said, grinning.

"My view just improved," Sinclair said, glancing over at her.

River bit her lip. She loved that Sinclair said things like that.

Sinclair held her arm out, and River moved to climb onto the bed, lying down with her head against Sinclair's shoulder.

"I couldn't sleep," she said.

"Yeah, me either," Sinclair said, cuddling her closer.

"This is going to be so hard…"

"Yeah…" Sinclair said, frowning in the semi-darkness of the room. "And I just need to make it easier."

River looked up at her. "What do you mean?"

"It's up to me to make it easier."

"Sin…" River said, sitting up, her look searching. "I'm not saying I won't do this—I will. I need you…"

Sinclair sat up too, capturing River's lips with hers, then pulled back to look at her.

"And I'm saying that I'm divorcing Tracey, because I need to be with you."

River's lips parted, her eyes reflecting her surprise. "I'm not saying—" she began.

"I'm not saying you are, babe," Sinclair said. "I'm saying that I want to divorce her and be with you. It's as simple as that."

"Sin, I don't want to be the reason for your divorce," River said, shaking her head.

"You aren't the reason for my divorce. Tracey and I are the reason for our divorce—hell, maybe it's me, I don't know… but I know that I don't love her anymore, and I do love you. So when she comes home I'm telling her I want a divorce."

"Are you sure about this?"

Sinclair nodded. "Completely."

She became even more sure two weeks later, when the group was over at the house to watch World Cup soccer. It was cold outside, so Sinclair was making her grandmother's potato soup, standing in the kitchen as the group watched the preliminaries, talking and drinking. It had been pre-decided that it was tequila day, so everyone had brought their favorite tequila and shots were abounding. Abe was happily ensconced on the couch, watching the match with Jericho, Kai, and Legend. Even Talon and Parker had shown up at Cat's urging.

Sinclair had had a number of shots and was drinking beer on top of that. She was chopping vegetables, and singing and dancing to whatever was on the stereo at the time. River was leaning against the counter, watching.

"Are you sure you should be that close to a really sharp knife when you've had as many as you have?" she asked, worried.

Sinclair grinned. "I'm fine, babe."

"Shots!" Quinn yelled.

"No!" River said, putting her hand over Sinclair's glass. "Sin needs to ease up here."

"No, Sin needs another shot," Sinclair said, leaning over to kiss River soundly while picking up her shot glass and holding it out to Quinn.

"You are so bad…" River said.

"Only in the best ways, baby," Sinclair said as she held up the shot and then drank it.

River just shook her head, grinning. She was happy to see Sinclair relaxing; the case was causing her a lot of headaches at that point. Tony had started to become incredibly suspicious of everything she did, and she was getting to the point of wanting to beat his head in, but remained cool. He'd asked a lot of questions about River; Sinclair had said that she had gone back east to visit family and that one of her relatives had taken sick, so she had stayed. She wasn't sure if Tony believed her or not. She'd warned River over and over again not to tell anyone where she was staying and not to go out of the house unless Sinclair was with her.

It was another hour, and a few shots later, that River leaned over to Sinclair.

"Uh, Sin…" she murmured, looking toward the living room.

"What?" Sinclair asked, following River's line of sight.

Tracey stood in the transition from the entryway to the living room, staring at all the people in the living room, her face like stone. She glanced over at Sinclair in the kitchen and walked in that direction. Her eyes fell on River as she approached.

"Wow, you didn't say you were coming home," Sinclair said evenly. She leaned on the counter, drinking a beer.

"I thought I'd surprise you," Tracey said. "I guess I was the one in for a surprise…"

Sinclair looked back at her, a half-grin on her lips. "Shit happens."

Tracey narrowed her eyes icily.

"You all remember Tracey, right?" Sinclair called to the group.

That was met with highly unenthusiastic "yeah"s and "uh-huh"s. Sinclair turned back to Tracey.

"Yeah, they remember you," she said, her smile overly sweet.

"I see."

Tracey's eyes strayed back over to River, who was still standing in the kitchen.

"Oh, this is River," Sinclair said. "She's my grandfather's nurse."

"So she'll be leaving with him when he goes home today?"

Tracey asked frostily.

"He is home," Sinclair said. "I moved him in here with us."

"I'm sorry?"

"Are you?" Sinclair replied, her look pointed.

"That's something we should have discussed," Tracey said, then glanced at River. "Do you think you could give us some privacy?" she asked sharply.

Sinclair's eyes narrowed. River saw it and nodded. "Of course," she said, and walked out of the kitchen.

Tracey watched her leave, her look measuring, then turned back to Sinclair.

"Tell me you're not fucking the help?" she said.

Sinclair stared back at Tracey, her expression unreadable. "Are you asking?"

"Are you fucking her?"

"How many women did you fuck while in Hong Kong, Singapore, or wherever the fuck else you've been?" Sinclair countered, with a little ice of her own.

Tracey glared back at her for a long moment, then shrugged. "They meant nothing."

"Well, see? That's worse, to me."

"What's that supposed to mean?"

Sinclair picked up her beer. "You know what? I have friends over, so I'm going to go back to my party now."

"You know I wanted to relax in my own house this evening."

"Then go buy your own fucking house," Sinclair said, and walked out of the kitchen.

Chapter 7

"That was a great homecoming," Tracey said the next day, when Sinclair finally dragged herself out of bed.

Sinclair ignored her and took off her clothes, walking into the bathroom and turning on the shower. She was hungover in the worst way, and the last thing she felt like doing was fighting with Tracey.

After her shower, Sinclair went into the kitchen and found that, mercifully, River had apparently made coffee. As she poured, she saw that River was out on the veranda. She walked outside, clutching her coffee, and sat in the chair next to River's.

River glanced at her and grimaced. She could see how horrendously hungover she was.

"I tried to get you to slow down," she said gently. "But after the talk with Tracey, you were just kind of done."

Sinclair nodded, taking a sip of her coffee. "Happens a lot these days," she said—softly, because her head hurt too much to talk in a normal voice.

"This might not be the best time to tell her, Sin…"

"Well, I'm not planning on it before I'm no longer hungover."

"Good," River said, grinning. "I better get inside before Abe wonders where I've run off to."

"How's he doing today?"

"Better." River smiled. "I think he really had a good time yesterday."

"Yeah, female attention, even lesbian attention, is awesome to him," Sinclair said, grinning. "I'll be down in a little bit to visit. Just gotta get ahead of this headache first."

"Try some aspirins."

"I was thinking tequila…"

"Oh, Lord," River said, rolling her eyes and shaking her head. "See you in a bit."

"Okay," Sinclair said, and watched River walk into the house, biting her lip.

Neither of them noticed Tracey on the stairs just below the veranda.

After a long visit with her grandfather, Sinclair went back to the master bedroom, intent on getting her laptop to do some work.

"So you are fucking her," Tracey said from her desk.

Sinclair turned around. She refused to lie about River. "Why are we still doing this?"

"What do you mean?"

"Jesus Christ, Tracey!" Sinclair exclaimed. "Why are you playing dense now?"

Tracey glared back at her icily. "What are you saying?"

"I'm saying I want a divorce."

Tracey stared at her for a long minute, then shook her head. "No."

"What?" Sinclair said, stunned.

"You heard me. We're not getting a divorce."

"Oh, we are," Sinclair said. "You can believe that."

"I won't sign anything."

"Good thing you don't have to in California," Sinclair said snidely.

"I see you've checked this out," Tracey said, narrowing her eyes. "I won't stop you from fucking the help, but you're certainly not leaving me for her."

"And that's where you're wrong."

"I'll fight you every step of the way."

"And I'll spend every penny I have to get out of this marriage," Sinclair snapped. "Oh, and you can move out too."

"Not going to happen. I'm not leaving my house."

"This isn't your house," Sinclair said. "It belongs to me. This house has been in my family since it was built! It's my house, and I want you out of it."

"So you can move your mistress in? Oh, wait, you already did."

"Well, I guess it's a good thing that adultery isn't a file-worthy offense, isn't it?" Sinclair said. "Then again, you admitted to doing it yourself, so…"

"You really can't prove that," Tracey said mildly.

"I'm a cop, you fucking idiot! You think I can't find evidence? You wanna try me? Really?"

"I'm not leaving."

"Well, you're not sleeping in here with me anymore, I can tell you that."

"I'll move into one of the guest rooms," Tracey said primly.

"Fine!" Sinclair snapped. With that, she walked out of the room, slamming the door.

River found her out on the veranda twenty minutes later, smoking, pacing, and drinking a beer, but not before she'd run into Tracey in the hallway and been given an icy stare.

"Jesus, what happened?" she asked, seeing how agitated Sinclair was.

"I told her I want a divorce and that I want her out of my house," Sinclair said, continuing to pace.

"And she's moving into the guest bedroom…"

"Yeah, 'cause she thinks she's going to fight me for everything," Sinclair said, narrowing her eyes.

"Oh, Sin…"

"It's fine, it's fine," Sinclair said, shaking her head. "It's just more shit I don't need right now, but that's why she's doing it."

"Sin…" River moved to stand in Sinclair's path, making her stop and look at her. "I don't want to cause you any more stress."

Sinclair stared at River. "You aren't causing me stress, babe. She is."

"But it's because of me."

"No, it's because she's a cunt!" Sinclair yelled toward the house.

River widened her eyes.

"What can I do?" River asked, reaching up to put her hands on Sinclair's shoulders.

Sinclair calmed immediately, looking down into River's green eyes. "Nothing, babe, except be here with me, okay?" she said softly.

River grimaced. "Are you sure she won't kill me in my sleep?"

"You'll be sleeping next to me, so I don't think so."

"Are you crazy?"

"Nope," Sinclair said, shaking her head. "She knows about you."

"You told her?" River asked, her eyes wide.

"She'd already figured it out. I just refused to deny it. I've lied about all I want to when it comes to you."

River stared up at Sinclair, tears in her eyes. "Sin…" she said softly.

"What?" Sinclair said, her eyes searching.

"I need to tell you something."

Sinclair widened her eyes, shaking her head. "Oh Lord…"

"No!" River said, laughing softly. "Nothing bad."

"Okay…"

"I just want you to know… that I love you."

Sinclair stared back at her for a long moment, closing her eyes slowly, then opened them again and smiled. "I love you too."

"You do?"

"Yeah. Why else would I risk blowing my cover to keep you with me?"

"You said for your grandfather…"

"'Cause I was too chickenshit to tell you the truth then. I was afraid you wouldn't ever forgive me for being married," Sinclair said. "I really did want you to be the one to be with my granddad, but the fact of the matter was, I just plain wanted to keep you in my life."

"Oh, Sin…" River said, putting her hand to Sinclair's cheek. "I would have stayed either way. I've loved you for a while now."

"Well, stay now."

"I plan to."

"Good."

Things between Talon and Parker stayed hot and heavy. When they weren't at Talon's condo, they were at the house in Long Beach. Talon preferred the condo, since they could be as loud as they wanted to be there, but she also found that she enjoyed spending time with Parker in the house as well, especially when she got to watch her with her grandbaby.

Filming for the movie had begun, so Talon was spending a lot of time commuting. She refused to stay at the condo alone at night, wanting to be with Parker as much as possible. One night filming went particularly late, and Talon hit traffic on the way out to Long Beach. She crawled into bed next to Parker at midnight. Parker immediately turned over, pulling her into her arms.

"How was filming, babe?" Parker asked.

"Long. Awful."

Parker kissed Talon's temple, stroking her back, as Talon rested her head against her shoulder.

"Get some rest, babe," Parker said.

Talon levered herself up on her elbow, looking down at her. "See? That's why I want to be with you."

Parker smiled bemusedly. "Uh-huh?"

"I tell you it was a long, awful day shooting the movie, and instead of a million questions about this, that, and the other thing, you just kiss me and tell me to get some rest." Talon shook her head. "Do you realize how amazing that is?"

"Uh, no?" Parker said, still confused.

"Every person I've ever dated wanted to know all about the movie business. I tell them I had a lousy day shooting a movie, they want details—Was Legend being too hard on me? Was my costar drunk, or high? Was there a problem with the script? On and on and on… It's exhausting. I mean, I would be exhausted already—"

"Which you are," Parker put in.

"Right, and then they'd want to talk for hours about how the movie business works, and it's so exhausting and I hate it—I hate it."

"And yet you're ranting about it instead of getting some rest," Parker said, grinning.

Talon looked back at her and started to grin herself. "Okay, never mind. I'm just going to shut up now," she said, moving to lie back down.

"I get it," Parker said, sliding her arm around Talon's shoulders again. "You're glad I'm not a groupie."

"Right!"

"Me too, babe. Me too."

Talon snuggled against Parker, enjoying having her arms wrapped around her. She knew she was getting herself addicted to this feeling, but she didn't care at that moment. It just felt so damned good to be there, and the feeling of Parker's heartbeat against her cheek soothed her.

The next day, Talon had a late call, and Parker had taken the morning off to be home with her. Talon woke Parker with her hands and mouth, exciting her beyond all reason. Fortunately, their room was far enough from Kim's to keep from waking her or the baby. Parker in turn spent extra time exciting Talon, which resulted in marks on Talon's skin that would mean the makeup artists on the film would be annoyed with her. Talon didn't care; she'd begun awakening Parker's wild side, and she loved everything that came with it. Parker had marks on her neck and body on occasion as well.

After making love a few times, Talon lay with her head in the hollow of Parker's shoulder, holding her hand.

"So how did you get into acting?" Parker asked.

Talon grinned. "Childhood trauma."

"You've said that before," Parker said soothingly. "Tell me what you mean."

Talon looked back at her, surprised by the request. "My parents... um... They kind of had a bit of a crazy response to my coming out..."

"Which was?"

"They sent me to a psychiatrist."

"Wow," Parker said, widening her eyes. "How much?"

"Like every day. They checked me into an institution for three months."

"Are you fucking kidding me?"

"Nope," Talon said, shaking her head.

"So… how does this involve you getting into acting?"

"How do you think I convinced them I'm straight?" Talon said, her green eyes sparkling mischievously.

Parker chuckled, shaking her head. "They probably know now, huh?'

Talon grinned. "Probably."

"I'll bet you were a handful for your parents."

"I definitely had my moments. I bought them a house to make it up to them."

Parker laughed. "Well, that's nice."

Later, after they'd got up and showered—and made love again in the shower—Talon watched Parker put her BDUs on for work.

"I want to go out to a nightclub with you," she said.

"Okay…" Parker said, looking over at her quizzically. "Why?"

Talon smiled evilly. "'Cause I want to get you in a dark corner…"

"No, not in public, Talon. I'm a cop, for God's sake."

"I know," Talon said, widening her eyes dramatically. "That's the exciting part about it."

"No," Parker said again, shaking her head.

"Okay, but go out with me."

"Where?"

"Somewhere the group isn't."

"Why?"

"You ask a lot of questions."

"It's a cop thing," Parker said, putting her foot up on the foot-board of the bed to tie her boots.

"I want you all to myself for a minute, okay?" Talon said, smiling.

"You have me all to yourself all the time, Tal."

"But not out at a nightclub, where there's music and dancing."

"Okay, fine," Parker said. "But make sure it's a Friday night so I have time to recover. I'm not quite the kid that you are."

"You keep up with me just fine where it counts," Talon said, smiling wickedly.

"Uh-huh," Parker said, leaning down to kiss her. "I'll see you tonight, beautiful."

"Be careful!" Talon called as Parker left the room.

"Always!" Parker called back.

Talon listened as Parker talked to Ginny, kissing her soundly, and then hugged Kim, telling her to have a good day. She bit her lip, thinking how nice it was.

Pictures of Talon Valois and her current girlfriend, Parker Gaines, showed up in every tabloid and regularly on TMZ. Parker had merely shaken her head about it, thanking God she wasn't undercover or anything. It was regularly noted that Talon looked extremely happy and seemed a bit more settled with Parker. The pictures showed Parker smiling at Talon, and the two of them kissing all the time.

Chelle Gaines threw the latest issue of the *Enquirer* across the office. Someone had been nice enough to leave it on her desk that morning. It irritated Chelle no end that Parker had chosen now to get interesting. She loved her, but she hadn't been able to resist the pull of a younger woman who had been enticing her for months. Now Parker was dating Talon Valois? What kind of horrible irony was that? Worse still, their daughter, the girl she had given birth to, seemed to absolutely love Talon. If Chelle dared to say one negative word about Talon, Kim would close up immediately. It was really annoying.

The fact was, she missed Parker. Yes, their life had gotten very boring and far too routine, but she missed their family, and she definitely felt like she was missing out on the new grandbaby. Kim was always talking about how Parker was the one that could always calm the baby down. It irked Chelle no end. She refused to admit, even to herself, that she missed the way Parker held her and looked at her. She also refused to think about the way that Parker might be looking at Talon Valois.

Talon made a point of looking particularly hot the Friday night she got Parker to go out. She wore a minidress of crushed velvet that laced up from her waist to the low neckline, leaving a lot of skin on display without really showing anything. The dress was a dusty pink color that was set off nicely by Talon's tan. She wore thigh-high velvet boots, her hair was loose and softly curled, and her makeup, as always, was perfect and soft.

Parker was ever astounded by this beautiful creature that saw fit to spend time with her.

"You look amazing," she said, smiling as she leaned in to kiss Talon.

"Let me see you," Talon said, looking Parker over and grinning.

She nodded. "You look hot."

"That's because you bought me half this stuff," Parker said, making a face.

"Because that femme you were living with obviously had a problem with color…"

"Who says she bought my clothes?"

Talon stared back at Parker for a long moment, her expression saying, *Really?* "She did the shopping for you, Parker. Don't even try to pull that with me."

Parker grinned. "You win that one."

Talon turned her toward the mirror. "Tell me you don't like the way you look in this."

Parker looked herself over in the mirror. She did have to admit she looked pretty good. She wore jeans and a black tank top made out of some kind of slithery material, and over that she had a turquoise, black and white flannel shirt completely open, with a black leather jacket that had a sweat material liner and hood. On her feet she wore Harley Davidson–style boots. Around her neck was a black leather thong with an onyx dog tag with a silver dragon head; Parker knew it was expensive, though Talon had refused to tell her how much it had cost—which was how Parker knew it was expensive.

"And the lady wins again…" Parker murmured as she grinned.

The outfit did look good, and it definitely wasn't something Chelle would have bought her. She thought it was interesting that Chelle thought she was boring, and was the one that bought her boring clothes. Talon saw her the way she wanted to see her—as exciting and sexy—and it was reflected in the clothes she'd bought her. There was a vast difference there, and Parker was seeing it more and more. She got an even better picture that night.

They were at another local lesbian bar, and Talon was dancing around to the music, even when they were standing at the bar. Parker watched her move and tried to fathom how she'd ended up with the beautiful little firefly. After a few shots, Parker was talked into dancing, which was something she wasn't normally given to doing. The alcohol and her incredibly hot girlfriend changed that quickly. They danced, they drank, they kissed heavily on the dance floor during slow songs. At one point, during a particularly hot, slow dance, Talon took Parker's hands, sliding them from the center of her back all the way down to her ass. Parker's eyes connected with hers as she noted the complete absence of a panty line of any type.

"Are you serious?" Parker asked, stunned.

Talon widened her eyes, smiling.

"Jesus…" Parker breathed as she leaned her head against Talon's shoulder, a sharp thrill going through her body.

Without a word, Talon took Parker's hand, leading her off the dance floor and into the women's bathroom, straight into the large handicapped stall. Talon barely had time to lock the door before Parker had her against the wall, kissing her deeply, pressing her body against her. Talon slid her hand up under the tank top Parker wore with no bra, touching hard nipples and moaning against her lips.

Parker gasped at the feel of Talon's hands on her, pressing herself closer, sliding her hands down and up under the dress, touching Talon and making her cry out. Talon moved her hands to Parker's shoulders to steady herself, her body alive with sensations. Parker pressed her harder against wall, then lifted her off her feet. Talon wrapped her legs around Parker's waist as Parker's fingers slid deep inside her. Talon had to press her face against Parker's neck as she cried out in her orgasm, sucking at Parker's skin. Afterward, she continued to move herself against Parker's fingers until she came again. She slipped one hand from Parker's shoulder, sliding it down into her tank top, fondling her nipple again and hearing Parker's sharp intake of breath.

Talon unwound her legs from Parker's waist, her heels making her an inch taller than Parker. She grabbed two handfuls of her jacket and turned her so that Parker's back was against the wall. She pushed the tank top up so she could put her mouth to a very hard nipple, sucking and biting slightly, making Parker jump and moan at the same time. Talon unbuttoned Parker's jeans and slid her hand down inside to touch her. Within moments Parker was coming against her hand, and doing her damndest not to make a lot of noise.

The music from the club pumped loudly into the bathroom, somewhat muffling the sound of them making love, but all it took was one person seeing them coming out of the same stall and the rumors started to fly. Within twenty minutes, it was known that Talon Valois and her paramour had been spotted having sex at a local nightclub. It didn't matter that no one had seen anything.

Unaware of the wagging tongues, Parker and Talon spent the rest of the evening dancing. Talon had a lot more to drink than Parker, who knew her limitations and as a cop always kept her wits about her. At one point Parker was sitting on one of the leather couches. Talon was next to her, her head on Parker's shoulder, her body pressed against her, both legs over Parker's thigh—literally as close to her as she could get. Parker held her protectively, stroking her neck and hair, reaching up to touch Talon's face tenderly with her other hand as she talked to her. Cameras captured every single moment.

"You okay?" Parker asked, aware that Talon was very drunk.

"Mmhmm," Talon murmured, nodding against Parker's shoulder and moving to nuzzle her lips against Parker's neck. "You smell so good."

Parker turned her head, kissing Talon's forehead tenderly. Talon smiled softly, loving the feeling of Parker's arm around her. She felt completely safe. She knew Parker would protect her no matter what. She also knew Parker had stopped drinking, to make sure she could do just that. She trusted her implicitly. She believed every move Parker made; she knew she never did anything for the cameras, for the fame, for the desire to sell her out. Parker was with her because she wanted to be with her, not to gain anything.

It was those thoughts that had Talon reaching up to grasp a handful of Parker's jacket, pulling at her.

"What is it, babe?" Parker asked, sensing Talon's sudden unrest.

Turning to face her, Parker took the girl's face in her hands, looking into her eyes. She could see that Talon was very drunk, but there was also something akin to desperation in her eyes.

"What is it?" she asked again.

Talon reached up, clasping at Parker's wrists. Parker pulled her into her arms. Talon held on to Parker's shirt, her head against her shoulder.

"Baby... talk to me," Parker whispered, her lips against Talon's ear.

Talon shook her head, suddenly feeling far too emotional. She knew it was the alcohol that was making her feel like this, and she didn't want to blurt anything out that she'd regret later. She pulled back, looking up into Parker's eyes, and touched her face, smiling.

"You are so incredible," Talon said.

Parker grinned. "And you are so drunk."

"That doesn't mean that I don't think you're incredible."

"Okay."

"You're humoring me."

"Yeah, I kind of am."

"I love that you always tell me the truth," Talon said, putting her arms around Parker's neck.

"Mmhmm," Parker murmured, signaling to a waitress for a bottle of water.

"Don't 'mmhmm' me, copper," Talon said, narrowing her eyes at Parker.

"Copper?" Parker said, chuckling. "There's one I haven't heard since… ever. Are you suddenly from the forties?"

"I'm an actress," Talon said, flipping her hair with flair. "I give the truth scope!"

"Huh?" Parker said, winking at the waitress as she handed her a bottle of water. She opened it and handed it to Talon. "Drink this."

"Why?" Talon asked.

"Because I said."

"What will you give me if I do?" Talon asked, her eyes sparkling.

"Anything you want," Parker said, widening her eyes slightly.

"Ohh…" Talon said, and lifted the bottle to her lips immediately.

Parker was lucky they made it home that night, since Talon decided to take the part about "anything" quite seriously and insisted on having sex in the back seat of the Cougar, which led to a very long session in a remote location in the hills.

Each night after Abe was asleep, River would walk upstairs and do her best to get past the guest bedroom without running into Tracey. She was usually successful—but she wasn't on this particular night. It was as if Tracey had been waiting for her.

"River, is it?" Tracey called from the desk in the guest bedroom.

River stopped mid-step, turning slowly to look at her. The woman would probably be considered handsome, except for the permanently dour look on her face and the fact that she was such a bitch, from what River had seen and heard in the last two weeks.

"How are you enjoying my bedroom?" Tracey asked mildly.

River stared back at her, not sure how she was expected to answer the question. She was, however, far from intimidated.

"Or, for that matter, how are you enjoying my wife?" Tracey continued. "Clair's pretty decent between the sheets."

"Decent?" River said, shocked. "I know you mean fucking amazing…"

Tracey shook her head. "I don't think so."

"Well, maybe that has everything to do with who she's having sex with," River said pointedly.

"Or lack of experience of the partner."

"Oh, I'm sure you have *some* experience."

Tracey gave her a wintery smile. "I've been a lesbian longer than you've been alive, little girl."

"Well, if you couldn't keep a woman like Sin satisfied, I'm thinking you didn't learn much over those years."

Tracey narrowed her eyes at her. River simply stared back, refusing to look away. She was damned if she was going to allow Tracey to talk shit about Sinclair, especially when it came to sex. She'd heard how unsatisfying the sex with Tracey had been, how staid and boring.

"You know, if you'd treated her better, you wouldn't be in this situation," River said.

"Treated her better?" Tracey repeated, as if the concept were beyond her grasp.

"Yeah, supported her in her career, and in who she is," River said. "Or did you only think that was her job?"

Tracey looked back at her, practically glowering.

"She didn't even need to work," she said. "But she insisted on doing that job, on becoming that... cover of hers!"

"She became who she really is, Tracey. You just don't want to see that. You want her to stay what you wanted, and that's not fair."

"Fair?" Tracey snapped. "You think it's fair that I married a girl and got a fucking guy?"

"You mean, like she got?"

Tracey opened her mouth to answer, and then her eyes went to the doorway behind River.

River glanced over her shoulder and saw Sinclair standing there,

191

leaning against the doorjamb, her blue eyes sparkling with interest.

"And what's going on here?" Sinclair asked.

"Your wife was trying to explain to me the finer points of satisfying a woman," River said, amused.

Sinclair's lips curled slightly. She reached out to River, taking her hand and leading her out of the room. Twenty minutes later, Tracey couldn't have missed the screams of pleasure from Sinclair if she'd been deaf; nor did she miss River's exclamations a few minutes later.

In the master bedroom, they lay together, Sinclair holding River in her arms.

"Think we proved our point?" Sinclair asked, grinning.

"Probably," River said, sighing happily. "But I really don't care—she really is a bitch…"

"Told ya."

"You were right."

Parker was out working with Kai and the new dog assigned to her, and things weren't going well. She hadn't realized how used to Bandit she'd become, and it was making it tough to transition to a new dog. She was finally making some progress when her phone rang. She let it go to voicemail.

"Sorry," she said to Kai, who gave her a pointed look. "I didn't realize it was no longer on vibrate." She took the phone out and changed the setting, and saw that it had been Chelle who called.

She then started to worry that it had been something to do with the baby, and found she couldn't concentrate. "Can we take a break?"

she asked. "I need to make a call."

"Sure. Back in ten, okay?" Kai said.

"Got it."

Parker called Chelle back.

"What's up?" she asked when Chelle answered.

"I, uh…" Chelle stammered. "I left you a voicemail."

"And you can't just tell me now?"

"Sorry, yes, of course. I just figured you were busy."

"I am, but what is it?" Parker said, leaning against the side of the building, crossing her legs at the ankles and reaching for a cigarette.

"Well, I was…" Chelle glanced down at the pictures of Parker and Talon at the club, and the headline reading *SEX IN LOCAL BAR, TALON VALOIS' LATEST ESCAPADE!* "Well, I was hoping we could talk."

"We are talking," Parker said, lighting the cigarette and taking a deep draw.

"I meant in person," Chelle said impatiently, scanning all of the pictures in the tabloid. She felt sick.

"Oh."

"Can we do that?"

"Yeah, okay," Parker said. "When?"

"Today?"

Parker blew her breath out. "I'm working right now. What about later, say four?"

"Okay. Can you pick me up from work?"

"Yeah."

"Okay, I'll see you then," Chelle said.

"Okay," Parker said, and hung up.

She finished her cigarette, wondering what bomb Chelle was getting ready to drop now. Maybe she was planning to marry… What was her name? Parker couldn't remember. Mary? Sherry? Shaking her head, she gave up trying to figure it out; she realized she didn't care anymore. Grinning, she went back to work.

Later that afternoon, Chelle was surprised to find Parker waiting for her outside her office building. She was leaning against the dark red Cougar she loved so much. Parker had a thing for all things "old classic," as she'd say. Chelle couldn't help but look her wife over— she definitely looked good. She was wearing tight-fitting black pants and a black V-neck T-shirt with a denim shirt over the top of it with the sleeves rolled up, exposing the tattoos on her forearms. She also wore a chain with a silver phoenix pendant with a blue center, matching the bracelet she wore over the black leather band on her wrist. There was no denying that her wife looked better now than she had previously. It irritated Chelle no end, because she knew it was Talon Valois' influence.

Walking up to Parker, Chelle reached up to hug her. She noted that Parker was very stiff as she accepted the hug.

"You're still allowed to hug me, you know," Chelle said, her tone reflecting her irritation. "I am still your wife."

She caught Parker's pursed lips and slightly narrowed eyes as she stepped back to let her open the passenger door for her. Parker seemed to forget for a moment to do just that, and then grinned even as she reached for the door.

As Parker started the car, "The Price of Love" by Bon Jovi came on. Chelle wondered if Parker had set it on the iPod on purpose. The song outlined an affair, talking about risking one's life for a stolen kiss. The chorus went, "We live, we learn, we lie, for the price of love." That was what she'd done. She'd lied to Parker for months, going behind her back with this younger woman. It had all seemed so exciting at the time. And she'd allowed herself to become someone else completely.

Chelle walked into the bedroom, surprised to find Parker home and lying on the bed.

"Hey," she said, doing her best not to look completely nervous and guilty.

"Hi," Parker said tiredly, her arm up over her eyes.

"Rough day?' Chelle asked as she started taking off her clothes, sure that she could still smell Terry on them and wondering if Parker would too.

"Just long."

"What time did you leave this morning?" Chelle had gotten all of her clothes off and was stuffing them in under other clothes in the hamper.

"Four thirty. You were out cold—I didn't want to wake you. Hey… is this an invitation?" Parker asked as she looked at Chelle, standing naked across the room.

Chelle forced a laugh, shaking her head. "No, I just got back from the gym. I need to shower."

"Maybe I'll join you," Parker said, grinning, as she sat up.

"No," Chelle said far too quickly. "I mean, it's too hard to shave my legs when there's two of us in there…"

"So you're shaving your legs, huh? That's usually a sign that I'm about to get lucky…"

"Not today, sailor," Chelle said. There was no way she could have sex with Parker after all the screwing around she and Terry had just done.

No way. In fact, Chelle was sure there was at least a mark or two on her that she'd need to hide from Parker for the next few days.

"I'm wearing a dress tomorrow—I can't be stubbly," she said by way of explanation, proud of herself for thinking of it.

It was another two weeks and a number of conversations with Terry later that Chelle left, feeling pulled away and just wanting to run back to Terry. She hated all the lying and sneaking around.

"Where've you been?" Parker asked when she walked into the kitchen. Her tone was far from accusing, but that was the way Chelle heard it. Everything sounded like an accusation these days, and Chelle knew it was the guilt that was killing her.

She sat down at the kitchen table. "We need to talk."

"Okay," Parker said. She had no idea what was coming.

"I want to separate for a while," Chelle said in a rush.

"Huh?" Parker looked completely stunned.

"I think we should separate."

"And why do you think that?"

"I just… Things have gotten really kind of… stale with us, and I

196

feel like I need to spread my wings."

Parker blinked a couple of times, her mouth open in surprise.

"Stale?" she finally managed to ask.

"Yeah," Chelle said. "I mean, it's the same old thing—work, dinner, talk about Kim, talk about the house, mediocre sex, and then bed..."

Parker stared back at her, her eyes narrowing slightly. "Mediocre sex."

Chelle dropped her eyes, shrugging. "You know, it's been... just... ordinary."

Parker chewed the gum in her mouth; she'd been trying to quit smoking again, because of Kim being pregnant, but this wasn't really helping that endeavor at this point.

"I see..." she said. "So you think separating will make the sex better?"

"I..." Chelle stammered. "I've met someone."

Parker looked like she'd actually slapped her—her mouth hung open, tears in her eyes. Her mouth worked in frustration and anger and just plain despair. She nodded, standing up from the table and walking out of the room. Chelle heard the front door slam and the Cougar start up a minute later then roar off down the street.

She sat staring into space for a few minutes. She hadn't expected Parker's reaction to be so strong—she'd actually convinced herself that Parker would be relieved.

Not only was Parker not relieved, she was devastated. When she finally came home, she moved around the house quietly, not entering the master bedroom at all. Chelle heard the guest bedroom door close a little while later. She lay in their bed that night relieved not to have to fight with Parker. They never fought. Parker's eyes took on a haunted look, but she never said another word. Chelle tried over and over again to talk to her, but Parker would just listen to whatever she said and nod, her face like stone, except for her eyes—her eyes always looked troubled.

The day Chelle moved out to be with her new twenty-two-year-old girlfriend, Parker stayed in the garage the entire time. Chelle went into the garage to try one last time to get something out of her.

"So, I'm leaving…" she said.

Parker continued to work on the car, nodding. The same thing she'd done for the last three weeks.

"You know, it's not like you couldn't have known this was coming. I mean, things have been so… boring. I mean… we just don't do anything exciting…"

Parker nodded again. If anything she seemed a little more devastated, but she wouldn't look at Chelle.

"Maybe you'll be happier," Chelle said.

That had Parker looking at her, her blue eyes reflecting anger now. Chelle could see that she was gritting her teeth, in the way the muscles in her jaw were jumping. But still Parker said nothing. She simply shook her head and went back to working on the car. Chelle huffed out of the garage then.

Chelle watched Parker, seeing that she even seemed to sit in her seat with more confidence now. *She's fucking a twenty-three-year-old superstar—who wouldn't be confident?* her brain screamed at her.

"I see that you've become rather famous lately," Chelle said, doing her best to keep the jealousy out of her voice, and not succeeding.

Parker glanced over at her, raising an eyebrow.

"Did you really have sex with her in a nightclub?" Chelle wanted to know, but also didn't want to know.

"I'm gonna plead the fifth on that one," Parker said, grinning.

"Which means yes," Chelle said, shaking her head. "I can't believe you did that..."

Parker chuckled. "It was actually pretty hot," she said, her eyes sparkling.

Chelle stared at Parker, shocked; this was not the woman she had been married to for twenty years. She shook her head.

"What?" Parker asked, aware that Chelle was having a hard time reconciling what she'd just heard.

"That's not you, Parker."

"Why do you say that?" Parker asked evenly.

"I've been married to you for two decades. I know you, and that's not you," Chelle said vehemently.

Parker looked thoughtful. "Maybe that's just not me with you," she said, her look pointed.

It was Chelle's turn to look like she'd been physically slapped, and Parker refused to feel bad about it. Chelle had leveled enough criticism at her in the three weeks after her admission of having an affair to deserve to hear a little bit of hard truth now.

Chelle drew in a deep breath, nodding as she expelled it slowly.

"I guess I deserved that," she said.

Parker didn't reply, just looked over at her as if to say, *Yes, you did.*

This was definitely not the Parker she was used to, at all. Parker had been the one that would do everything in her power to keep things from hurting Chelle, physically and emotionally. Now she was actually saying things that she knew would hurt her.

"What is she doing to you?" Chelle asked, affronted.

"Nothing that your own twenty-two-year-old isn't doing to you."

"She's not getting me to have sex in public, Parker," Chelle snapped.

"Sorry, I thought she was so 'adventurous'—isn't that one of the things you told me about her? That she liked to *try* things?" Parker said, her own ire coming to bear now.

"Is that what this is about? Getting me back? One-upping me?"

"No," Parker said. "I don't have to try and keep up with a twenty-two-year-old checkout girl, thanks."

Chelle stared, openmouthed. "You investigated her?"

"I'm a cop, that's not too hard to figure."

They were both silent for a couple of minutes.

"Anyway, what did you want to talk about?" Parker asked.

Chelle was silent, not sure if she was brave enough to say it now.

"I guess it's safe to say that you don't really miss me," she said eventually, sighing.

"That's a safe statement, yes."

Chelle nodded, chagrined. "I miss you, Parker."

"Yeah? What do you miss?"

"Our life, our house... our daughter."

"You can still see our daughter, you just have to leave Bambi at home."

"Her name is Terry."

"Whatever," Parker said, nonplussed. "What do you miss about our life? If I recall correctly, you said our life was stale and boring... or was that just the sex? I can't remember..."

Chelle realized she'd really managed to hurt her wife, and knew it had been sheer stupidity on her part that had allowed her to do that. Part of her had thought Parker was impervious to being hurt; she always took everything in her stride. She had seemed to take the affair in her stride too, but apparently that had been a carefully constructed facade. Chelle tended to believe now that had she really been paying attention, she'd have known how badly she was hurting Parker, but the fact was, at that point she hadn't cared.

"I'm sorry," she said, shaking her head. "I know I said a lot of things that were..."

"Shitty," Parker supplied when Chelle trailed off.

"Yes," Chelle said. "I'm sorry about that."

"Yeah, well, that doesn't erase it from my mind."

Chelle nodded. "I guess taking it all back won't help, huh?"

"Not even close," Parker said, shaking her head.

"So asking you for another chance is crazy too?" Chelle said tremulously.

Parker glanced over at her sharply, the look in her eyes reflecting her shock. She looked back out at the road, then at her hands on the steering wheel, then back out at the road.

"I don't know if I can do that," she said, shaking her head.

"Because of her?"

"Because of you," Parker said, her look accusing. "Because you shredded my trust in you. Because you blindsided me completely. Blaming Talon for what you've done to our marriage may be the thing that helps you sleep at night, but you need to remember that I know who broke us, Chelle, and it was you."

Chelle stared back at her, surprised by what she'd said, but also realizing she was completely right about all of it. It had made the guilt lessen when she'd seen Parker with Talon Valois; somehow it had convinced her that it was Talon's fault Parker wasn't beating down her door to get her back.

"Do you love her?" she asked, swallowing convulsively as she waited for the answer.

"You don't have the right to ask me that."

Chelle pressed her lips together, nodding.

"Do you still love me?" she asked.

Parker didn't answer, her look contemplative, then shrugged. "I don't know," she said simply.

It was far from what Chelle wanted to hear.

"She actually wants you back?" Talon asked, shocked. "Why, because she's jealous?"

Parker shrugged. "Or maybe she's realized that a twenty-two-year-old is far from her speed."

"Really?" Talon said, moving to straddle Parker's lap. "What about me? Am I far from your speed?" she asked as she leaned down to kiss her.

"Oh yeah…" Parker said, her hands sliding over Talon's hips as she pulled her closer.

"Mmm…" Talon murmured against Parker's lips. "Why don't you show me your speed, handsome…"

They were making love minutes later, and Talon was fairly certain Parker was very much up to speed.

Chapter 8

Late fall in Los Angeles began to suck when it rained for two weeks straight. It made a mess out of traffic; there were constant snarls due to accidents. Streets were flooded, people were on edge. Life was hectic.

One particularly nasty, stormy night, Parker had just made it home. She was on her cell phone as she walked inside, having been trying to get ahold of Talon since she'd left the office. She wanted her to stay at her condo that night because she didn't want her trying to drive all the way to Long Beach in the pouring rain. Talon wasn't answering, which had Parker worried.

She'd no sooner hung up than her phone began to ring, just as she got into the house. Glancing at the display, she saw that it was Chelle. She considered not answering it, but that wasn't her style, avoiding people.

"Hey, Chelle, what's up?" she said, her tone businesslike.

"Parker…" Chelle said, nearly hysterical. It made the hair on the back of Parker's neck stand up.

"What's wrong, Chelle?"

"My car went off the road—I think a tire blew. I'm in a ditch."

Parker took a slow, deep breath against the panic that wanted to rise.

"Okay, where are you?" she asked, putting her hand over the

mouthpiece of her phone as she whistled for Bandit; he came at a run. She walked back out into the garage, Bandit at her heels. She grabbed a few things off the shelf, including a crowbar, and put everything into the trunk of the Cougar, including her gear bag. She gestured for Bandit to get in the back before climbing in herself and backing out of the garage.

"Um… I don't know for sure—I was just driving," Chelle was saying, clearly panicked. "Parker, there's water in the ditch. It's high. I—I'm scared."

"Okay, stay calm, Chelle. I'm coming, okay. Tell me where you were."

"I was on East Ocean Boulevard going north. I turned, though… um…" Chelle said, trailing off as her breathing became faster and faster.

"Chelle, I need you to calm down," Parker said, her voice calm and soothing. "Think back to where you were. Did you pass Rosie's Dog Beach—you know, where I used to exercise Bandit?"

She heard Chelle breathe out slowly. "Yes, I passed that."

"Okay, how much longer did you drive before the tire blew?" Parker was now heading west toward Ocean Boulevard; thankfully she didn't need to get on any freeways.

"Um… I… like, five minutes."

"Okay…" Parker said, thinking hard. Fortunately, she traveled Ocean Boulevard fairly often, so she knew the area. "Did you pass the museum?"

"Yes, I think so. It's raining so hard!" Chelle said, her voice rising in panic again.

"Calm down, Chelle. I'm on Ocean now, I'll be there soon. I just need to know where I'm going, okay? You said you turned—when did you turn? And did you go right or left?"

"Uh… I went left, because it was flooding near the park."

"That park you used to do yoga in?"

"Yeah, yeah, exactly!"

"Okay," Parker said. "Honey, I got you. You're still driving the Honda, right?"

"Yes," Chelle said, her breathing getting fast again.

"Chelle, I'm coming, okay? I'll be there really soon. Are you hurt?"

"I—I don't think so," Chelle said, sounding like she was trying to decide.

In another couple of minutes Parker was turning onto Junipero and slowing down, because it was pouring with rain and it was hard to see.

"Right, I'm on Junipero. I'm sending Bandit to find you."

"Okay."

"Just stay on the line, okay?"

"Okay," Chelle said again.

Parker pulled over to the side of the road, then let Bandit out and knelt down in front of him.

"Suche Chelle!" she said—the search command.

Bandit put his nose up and took off. Parker stood up, putting her phone in her breast pocket, then reached into the trunk to grab her gear before following him. It only took Bandit a couple of minutes to find the car. It was sideways in the ditch, and Parker could see where it had skidded off the road.

"Sitze!" Parker ordered Bandit; he did, whining slightly.

"It's okay, boy, good job!" Parker said, rubbing his head. "I'll take it from here."

Parker half climbed, half slid down the low embankment. There was indeed water rising in the deep ditch. She needed to get Chelle out of the car. Chelle waved frantically as Parker tried to pull the door, but it wouldn't budge.

Parker took out her phone. "Is there water in the car?"

"Yes," Chelle said. "On the passenger side"

"Okay, I'm going to try the door again. Can you try pushing from your side?"

"Yes, okay."

"Right, count of three," Parker said, hitting speaker on her phone and putting it in her pocket again. She braced against the bottom and side panels of the car, gripping the door handle. "One, two, three!" she yelled.

She yanked on the door, but still it wouldn't budge.

"I'm gonna have to try prying it," she said, dropping the bag and getting out the crowbar.

She jammed it into the door frame and levered it down toward the car, hearing a shriek of metal as the door gave a bit. Repositioning the crowbar, she threw all her weight against it and felt the door give completely. In minutes she was reaching in to grab Chelle's hand to pull her out. All the while Bandit barked excitedly. Parker tossed the bag up to the road and then scrambled up the embankment. She lay on the ground on her belly, reaching back down for Chelle and pulling her up the incline.

When they got to Parker's car, Parker opened the passenger door, seeing her in safely, then got Bandit into the back seat. She put the bag back in the trunk and then got in. She grabbed the blanket off the back seat and put it around Chelle's shoulders, then pulled off her jacket to lay it over her legs. She started the car and got the heat going as quickly as she could.

"Are you hurt at all?" she asked Chelle again.

"No," Chelle said. "Thank you, Parker. I don't know what I would have... Thank you," she said, her teeth already chattering.

"It should be warm soon, okay?" Parker said, searching Chelle's face.

Chelle nodded. "Parker, you're soaked though. You should take this," she said, starting to lift the blanket off her.

"If it's not on you, it's going on Bandit, so keep it," Parker said with a grin as she flipped a U-turn to leave.

Chelle laughed softly. "Sorry, Bandit," she said, grinning at the dog.

"Look, are you okay with going back to the house? I don't want to try getting you all the way across town in this," Parker said, gesturing to the rain and wind outside.

"That's fine," Chelle said, nodding. "I really don't want you or I to be out in this any more than we already have been. Are Kim and the baby there?"

Parker grinned. "Yeah, Kim's completely freaked about the storm."

"Still?" Chelle said, smiling too.

Kim had always been afraid of storms. Wind and rain scared her, and they'd always ended up with the girl in their bed every time there was a storm. Fortunately, California wasn't given to many of them. It surprised Chelle that Kim still hadn't grown out of that fear.

"Oh yeah," Parker said, rolling her eyes.

"She is rather special, our daughter," Chelle said.

"That's a safe statement."

As she drove, Parker pulled her phone out, hitting redial then speaker and setting it in its cradle. Chelle could see that the display said "Talon"; she did her best to push down the jealousy she instantly felt. The phone rang and rang, then went to Talon's voicemail. Parker grimaced and hung up.

"Damnit…" she muttered, shaking her head.

"Problems?" Chelle asked, hoping she didn't sound too overly optimistic.

Parker heard it anyway and glanced over at her, her look telling Chelle she had, then shook her head.

"I haven't been able to get ahold of her," she said, reaching over to stab at the display on the phone, trying to split her attention between that and driving.

"How about you keep your eyes on the road and I'll dial whatever you need?" Chelle said as she reached for the phone, shifting a little closer on the bench seat.

Parker chuckled. "Okay. Look up Legend in my contacts."

"Okay," Chelle said, opening Parker's contact list; it was a lot longer now, she noticed. She saw names like Cat, Dakota, Devin,

Harley, Jazmine, Jericho, Jet, and Kashena as she scrolled through to find Legend.

"Legend Azaria?" she asked, shocked.

Parker nodded, grinning. "You do remember Talon's a movie star, right?"

"How could I forget..." Chelle murmured as she touched the name and the contact information came up.

"Well, she's working on another picture with Legend right now," Parker explained. "Can you hit call?"

"Of course," Chelle said, doing so and putting the phone on speaker.

Legend answered quickly.

"'Lo?"

"Legend, it's Parker."

"Hey, what's up?"

"Did you guys wrap for the day?"

"Yeah, like three hours ago," Legend said. "Why?"

"I can't get ahold of Talon."

"Well, she's probably stuck in traffic, like me. It's murder, trying to get to Malibu at this point, so I'm imagining Long Beach is just as hard."

"Yeah, but she's not answering her phone. I'm hoping she's staying at the condo tonight."

"Good luck with that," Legend said, grinning. "She's always moody when she doesn't stay with you—I've basically asked her to stop staying overnight wherever you're not."

Parker laughed. "Hadn't heard that," she said, shaking her head.

"Keep trying her phone, Park. She's probably just listening to her music at such a volume that she can't hear it."

Parker sighed, thinking Legend was probably right but not willing to settle until she got ahold of Talon and knew for sure.

"Okay, thanks. You drive safe out there, huh?"

"You too," Legend said. "Later!"

"Bye."

Chelle disconnected the call.

Parker blew her breath out, shaking her head. "Just put it back in the cradle. Legend's probably right. I'm gonna kill her..." she muttered.

"You've got a lot of names in your contact list now..." Chelle said, trailing off as she realized it wasn't really any of her business—but it bugged her that the names all sounded like women's.

"Mostly the group," Parker said.

"The group?"

"Friends I've made over at DOJ and the people they hang out with."

Chelle nodded, surprised. Parker wasn't usually very social. Yet another change in her.

They were both silent for a bit, then Parker's phone began ringing, and Chelle could see it was Talon.

"Finally!" Parker exclaimed, hitting the display to answer the call. "Where have you been!"

"In fucking traffic for like three hours!"

"What freeway are you on?"

"I'm on the 710 now, but the 101 was murder."

"So you're coming to the house then?"

"Uh, yeah, that was my plan. Why?"

"I was just thinking you'd maybe stay at the condo tonight since it's so bad out."

"Well, I hadn't planned on it…" Talon said, trailing off. "You sound like you're in the car—are you coming up here?"

"No, I had… well…" Parker said, glancing over at Chelle. "I kind of had to rescue Chelle from a ditch, so…"

"You what?" Talon exclaimed. "Are you okay?"

Chelle noted that Talon didn't ask about her, just wanted to know that Parker was okay. Nice…

"I'm fine, just wet as all get out," Parker said, grinning.

"Where are you?" Talon asked.

"Headed back to the house. Chelle's with me," Parker said, making sure Talon was aware that Chelle could hear whatever she said—not that it would matter to Talon one bit.

"Oh, yeah, then I'm definitely coming to the house tonight," Talon said, her tone reflecting the narrowing of her eyes.

Parker couldn't help the grin that spread across her lips. "Okay, just drive carefully, please."

"Oh, you bet," Talon said, an edge to her voice.

"Tal…" Parker said. "Do not let that temper of yours get the better of you—we don't need another fender bender to deal with."

"Hey, that last one wasn't my fault," Talon said, grinning.

"Yeah, that'll be up to the courts to decide," Parker said, laughing.

"Yeah, yeah. I'll see you soon, babe."

"Okay, see you soon," Parker said, then disconnected the call.

Chelle was able to stay silent for a full minute before she had to say something.

"So she's worried about me being at the house?" she asked, more sharply than she'd meant to.

Parker glanced over at her, her look pointed. "She tends to be... uh..."

"Territorial?"

"Well, yeah," Parker said, grinning.

"So you told her about our conversation?"

"Did you think I wasn't going to?" Parker stared at Chelle like she was crazy if she'd thought that.

Chelle sighed, shaking her head. "No, you're far too honest for that, aren't you?"

Parker simply nodded.

"So this ought to be fun..." Chelle said, having not thought about the fact that Talon would likely be at the house.

In truth, she'd hoped that Talon wasn't around most of the time, being a busy movie star and all. When Parker had suggested that she stay at the house that night, part of Chelle had hoped it was an opportunity. Now she realized it *was* an opportunity, but not the kind she'd hoped for—it was a chance for her to witness how Talon and Parker really were together. Chelle secretly hoped their relationship wasn't as rosy as the tabloids made it out to be.

Two hours later, that hope was completely dashed. Chelle, Parker, Kim, and Ginny were all settled in the living room, because Kim was completely freaked out by the storm. Chelle had just drifted off to sleep when Talon walked into the house. Pretending to be asleep, Chelle watched furtively from the couch as Talon walked over to where Parker slept on another couch. Talon knelt down, leaning over to kiss Parker's lips, reaching up to touch her face.

Parker opened her eyes. "Hey, babe," she said softly, mindful of everyone else sleeping in the room. "Finally made it?"

"I hate LA," Talon said, grinning.

"Uh-huh," Parker said, grinning too.

"I'm going to go grab a shower and change, okay?"

"Okay."

Half an hour later, Talon lay down on the couch next to Parker, facing her. Chelle noticed that Parker's arms went around her immediately, holding her close, and that Talon seemed to snuggle right into Parker. It was obviously something they did regularly. They kissed for a while, and things got a little bit heated, but Parker broke it off, grinning.

"Behave yourself," she murmured.

"You know I suck at that," Talon whispered back.

"Uh-huh..."

Talon sighed loudly, then shifted to put her back against Parker's chest, her left hand reaching out to clasp Parker's right, since Parker's right arm was under her neck. They lay like that for a while, Talon's fingers sliding over Parker's over and over again.

"What's this?" Talon asked softly, touching a cut at the base of Parker's thumb.

"Skip did it."

Skip was the pit bull Parker was working with.

"Ouch," Talon said, bringing Parker's hand up to her lips and kissing the wound gently.

"Yeah, he got a little grabby with his toy."

"How's that going?" Talon asked, aware that Parker had been having a rough time adjusting to the new dog.

Parker sighed. "Slow, very slow. We're just not clicking."

"Do you need a different dog, maybe?"

"I don't know. I'm thinking about bringing Skip home with me to try and bond better with him."

"How's Bandit going to feel about that?"

"Yeah, that's part of my concern," Parker said. "That and how Kim'll feel about a pit around Ginny."

Talon sighed. She knew it was really bothering Parker that things weren't going well with her new K9. Turning her head, she kissed Parker's upper arm.

"I'm sorry," she said softly.

Parker nuzzled Talon's neck in response, appreciating that she understood what she was going through and that it was rough. Talon reached up to touch Parker's head affectionately. Parker nuzzled closer, and Talon's hand dropped behind her to touch her sweats-clad thigh, rubbing over it and then reaching back to pull her closer, moaning softly.

"What part of 'behave yourself' do you not understand?" Parker whispered against her ear, even as she grinned.

Talon was now rubbing and grasping at Parker's thigh, sliding her hand back to grasp the curve of her ass, and it was definitely getting uncomfortable for Parker. The girl was far too sensual for her own good.

"Oh, I understand it. I just can't really manage it around you," Talon replied, pressing herself back against Parker.

"Tal... I swear..." Parker muttered as she started to chuckle, her body already trembling.

"We could go in the other room..."

"Or you could just behave yourself..."

Talon sighed, holding up her hand in surrender.

"Fine," she said, smiling, then put her right hand in Parker's and pulled her arm around her tightly.

Parker settled against Talon, her arms wrapped around her, her head lowered to her neck. They fell asleep that way.

Chelle lay on the other couch, knowing without a doubt she wasn't ever getting Parker away from Talon and hating the woman for it.

They were all asleep when the baby started crying. Kim got up as everyone woke up. She picked Ginny up, trying to cuddle her, then tried feeding her and checking her diaper. Chelle had gotten up by that time and tried to hold Ginny too. Parker and Talon watched from the couch. Ginny wouldn't stop crying.

"Mom, maybe you should try," Kim said, looking at Parker.

"Okay, give her to me," Parker said to Chelle.

Talon moved to sit up as Chelle walked over to hand the baby down to Parker, who still lay on her side.

"What's all this?" Parker said softly to Ginny, who had big croc-odile tears in her eyes. "This is not authorized," she said, smiling at the baby, touching her chin.

To everyone's surprise, Ginny quieted instantly, staring up at Parker.

"See? That's much better, isn't it?" Parker said, smiling, glancing at Kim and Chelle to see them staring openmouthed at her. "What?"

"You have the touch," Kim said, smiling.

"Uh-huh," Parker murmured, sounding unconvinced.

She reached up, touching the baby's fingers. Ginny immediately wrapped her hand around Parker's finger and tried to put it in her mouth.

"Hey, don't eat that," Parker said, grinning, even as the baby succeeded in getting her finger into her mouth. "Uh, I think she might be teething," Parker added, touching the baby's gums. "Yeah, definitely teething."

"What do I do about that?" Kim asked. "She's only four months!"

"You teethed early," Chelle said.

"I did?"

"Yep," Parker said, grinning as she exchanged a look with Chelle. "Okay, grab one of those cloth diapers, and then grab one of my hair ties off the dresser. Put an ice cube in the middle of the diaper and then put the hair tie around the whole thing. Then bang the ice cube on the counter."

"Um…" Kim said, looking confused.

"Trust me," Parker said.

Chelle nodded to Kim. "She knows what she's talking about."

Kim did as Parker had told her, then handed the diaper to her. Parker removed her finger from Ginny's mouth and gave her the end of the diaper with the crushed ice in it. Ginny chewed on it happily.

"Wow," Kim said. "I would have never guessed that one."

"That's why it's handy to have Grandma around," Chelle said, winking at Parker.

Talon watched the exchange and felt a tug at her heart. She knew Parker and Chelle had shared a lot over the years. Twenty years of raising a daughter and being together. How was she ever going to compete with that? It was a thought that nagged at her.

Sinclair woke with River in her arms, and lay doing her best to soak in the moment. She was headed back out to her undercover work that morning, and knew she'd miss having River in her arms. Regardless, she was happy to know that the worst thing that would happen to River while she was gone was that she'd have to deal with Tracey. Tracey was, however, leaving for Hong Kong in three days, so it wouldn't even be a long sentence for River.

River stirred, looking up at Sinclair and seeing that she was awake.

"Good morning," she said, stretching and sliding her hand up Sinclair's chest fondly.

"Morning," Sinclair said, smiling.

"How long have you been awake?" River asked, glancing at the clock; it was still early.

"Not long."

River bit her lip. "You're going back today, aren't you?"

Sinclair hadn't said, but River had sensed that she was gearing up mentally. She'd been lost in thought frequently the past few days.

Looking down at River, Sinclair nodded.

River pressed her lips together. She knew it was what Sinclair did for a living, and if she was going to be with her it was something she'd have to get used to, but it didn't make her less afraid at that moment. Moving to kiss Sinclair's lips, River used her body to show her that she loved her and that she'd miss her. She did everything she could to push down the fear she felt.

When they both lay breathless on the bed, Sinclair holding River, they both stared out at the view, each lost in their own thoughts as the wind and rain raged outside.

"I love you," River said, her head against Sinclair's shoulder, her hand on Sinclair's stomach.

"I love you," Sinclair said, putting her hand up to caress River's neck.

"I'm going to miss you."

Sinclair grinned. "Yeah, this is going to suck."

River laughed softly, nodding. Then she moved to sit up, looking at Sinclair.

"You'll be careful though, right?"

"I'm always careful, River."

River nodded, doing her best not to look as afraid as she felt.

They got up a little while later, and Sinclair showered and dressed. When she walked out to the kitchen, she noted that Tracey was sitting across from where River stood sipping her coffee. They were staring at each other, and Sinclair could almost feel the electricity in the room.

Tracey's eyes went to Sinclair as she walked in, looking completely butch with her hair back in a ponytail, jeans, boots, black tank, and jean jacket.

"Well, there's the butch that you love so much…" Tracey said derogatorily.

River walked over, leaning up to kiss Sinclair, then handed her a coffee and went back to lean against the counter.

"That's the difference between you and me, Tracey. I love her no matter who she is."

Sinclair's lips curled in a grin as she sipped her coffee.

Before she left, she went down to see her grandfather. She'd spent many hours with him in the last week. She sat next to him on the bed.

"Hey, I'm gonna be gone for a few days, okay," she said, leaning in to kiss his cheek.

"Where you goin'?" Abe asked.

"Work, Dad."

"I wish you'd go into the movies, Sinclair Marie."

"You know that's not me," Sinclair said, shaking her head. "I'm good at what I do."

Abe nodded, not looking happy.

"River's gonna be here with you, okay?" Sinclair said.

"You love that girl, don't you?"

Sinclair smiled softly, lowering her eyes. "I do, yeah."

"What are you going to do about that wife?"

"I'm trying to divorce her."

"Don't just try to do it, Sinclair," Abe said, narrowing his eyes.

"She's fighting me."

Abe looked displeased by that information, but nodded unhappily. "I like River," he said.

"I know."

"She reminds me of your grandmother."

"I know," Sinclair said, grinning. "Hands off, Dad—she's mine."

Abe laughed softly. "If you insist."

An hour later, River walked Sinclair out to the Challenger. She hugged her, resting her head against her chest.

"Please, please, please be careful," River said softly.

"I will, babe," Sinclair said, leaning down to kiss her lips. She pulled back. "I love you."

"I love you. Please drive carefully in all this mess."

A couple minutes later, Sinclair climbed into the Challenger and backed out of the garage. Leaving the house, she carefully checked around the area and went around two or three back streets to make she wasn't being followed. When she was confident that no one was observing her, she crossed Sunset and headed south.

An hour later she walked into her UC apartment. She hated it, but was determined to wrap up this case. She made a few calls, check-ing in with her contacts.

Later that night, she met with Tony.

"Where've you been, Sinclair?" he asked, shaking his head.

"I told you, I had some shit to handle down south."

"So your shit is handled now?"

"Yep, all buttoned up."

"So what happened to that nurse you were datin'? What was her name—like, Ocean or something."

"River?" Sinclair said, looking nonchalant. "I heard she went back east or something, some family thing."

"Same time you were gone?"

Sinclair shrugged. "How do I know? I don't track the girl's every movement."

"Eddie said you two were a thing."

"Eddie talks a lot of shit. He wanted her for himself."

Tony laughed. "Yeah, but she had a job that wasn't layin' on her back!"

Sinclair laughed too. Eddie's predilection for hookers was well known.

"So where do we stand?" she asked, getting down to business and wanting the topic off River.

Tony looked thoughtful for a long moment, then nodded. "We gotta meet down south in three days. Hopefully this shit rain'll stop by then."

"Yeah," Sinclair said.

Three days later, not only had the rain not let up, it had gotten much worse. As Sinclair drove the Challenger south on I-5, she decided to make a quick call. She was alone, meeting Tony later that day.

River answered on the second ring. "Hi!"

"Hey, I'm on my way south," Sinclair said. "Just thought I'd check in."

"Should you be calling?"

"I'm alone, and I'll make it quick. They set the meet for somewhere like a fuckin' mile from the border, it's ridiculous. We're probably going to drown out here in fuckin' Otay," she added, grinning.

"I love you, just drive carefully."

"Love you, will do," Sinclair said, disconnecting a moment later.

River stood outside on the covered veranda that led from the master bedroom. She'd spent the night lying with her face on the pillow Sinclair usually slept on, for the third night in a row. She missed Sinclair like crazy, but the phone call had cheered her up and she knew that was exactly why Sinclair had done it.

Picking up her phone, she dialed Cat's number.

Cat answered on the third ring. "Roché," she said absently as she studied a report on her desk.

"Cat, it's River. I wanted to let you know that Sinclair called me."

"From her cover?" Cat asked, instantly worried.

"Yeah, she said she was alone. Anyway, I wanted to tell you that she's headed south. She said they had a meet like right by the border or something."

"By the border?"

"That's what she said."

"I don't like that," Cat said, shaking her head.

"Why?" River asked, suddenly worried.

"It's too easy for them to make her disappear if they've made her…" Cat said without thinking about who she was talking to, then realized it when River sucked her breath in sharply. "Shit, River, I'm sorry," Cat said, grimacing. "It'll be fine—Sinclair knows what she's doing. I'm just being paranoid," she added, even as she messaged Raine and one of her other people on the computer, telling them to get to her office *now*.

River nodded, but couldn't help feeling sick.

Two days later no one had heard from Sinclair. River was beside herself. Cat had sent word through Sinclair's service to contact her. She hadn't responded. Cat was worried now too. She'd reached out to every connection she had to see if they'd heard any chatter. Jet had pressed every informant she had. They were getting nowhere fast.

Cat went to see River at the house.

"What exactly did she say that day she called you?"

"She said that the meet was like a mile from the border," River said tremulously. "She said something about drowning in 'oh-tie'—I didn't get what that meant."

"Wait, she said Otay?" Cat asked. "That's how she said it?"

River nodded. "Yes."

"Fuck! Right, just hold tight, okay? I gotta get a bird." Cat got on her cell phone immediately, calling Shenin. "Shen, I need a bird."

"You think you have a lead on Sinclair?" Shenin asked.

"Yeah."

"Okay, what do you need?" Shenin opened her computer; she was sitting on her bed with Tyler.

"I need something like a C-26… and I need FLIR," Cat said—a Forward Looking Infrared.

"Jesus…" Shenin breathed. "You're looking for her body?"

"I'm looking for a live body, Shen," Cat whispered, turning away from River.

"I'm on it. I'll let you know how soon I can get one. In the meantime, have you thought of the K9s?"

"That's a good idea too—I have an idea of where we're searching. Think I can get a bird to fly them down? Maybe Sky with a copter?"

"You got it. I'm on it."

Cat's next call was to Kai. "I need you," she said the moment Kai answered.

Kai grinned. "I don't know how Fin's gonna feel about that."

"I'm serious, Kai. I need you and Digger."

"Okay," Kai said, serious instantly. "This about Sinclair?"

"Yeah," Cat said. "Can you grab Parker too, and her dog?"

"You got it. Where do you want us?"

"Hit the Long Beach airport. I'm getting a chopper to take you down to San Diego."

"We'll be there inside the hour," Kai said, glancing at Finley as she walked into the room.

"Thanks," Cat said.

"What's up?" Finley asked as Kai dialed Parker's number.

"Cat thinks she has a lead on Sinclair," Kai said, putting her phone up to her ear.

Parker answered on the second ring. "Hey, Kai, what's up?"

"We need you and Bandit."

"Sinclair?" Parker asked immediately.

"Yeah," Kai said. "Meet me at the Long Beach airport as soon as you can."

"I'll beat ya there."

"What's going on?" Talon asked as Parker started to change clothes.

"They think they have a lead on where Sinclair might be," Parker said.

"They're sending you?"

"And Bandit."

"Jesus…" Talon said. "They're looking for her body, aren't they?" She looked terrified. "They think she's dead."

Parker stepped over to her, pulling her into her arms. "I hope not. But it's a definite possibility. She hasn't made contact in two days—it doesn't look good."

Talon gripped Parker's shirt, fighting back tears. She'd only met Sinclair a couple of times, but it always worried her when an officer was hurt. She understood it now because she was dating one.

226

"You be careful down there," she said.

"Always, babe," Parker said, kissing her temple.

"What's happening?" River asked Cat.

Cat glanced back at her and saw how worried she was. She wasn't sure that what she had to tell her was going to help, but she needed River to be prepared.

"I think I know where the meet was taking place. There's an area called Otay Mesa in San Diego, right next to the border. There's a lot of brushland out there, and if they were doing anything dirty that's where they'd do it. So I'm getting a plane with FLIR—it's infrared that can find a heat signature. I'm also calling out Kai and Parker with their K9s. If she's out there, River, we'll find her."

"Do you think she's alive?" River asked, her voice trembling.

"I don't know," Cat said, shaking her head. "I'm hoping, but I really don't know."

River nodded, tears sliding down her cheeks.

"I need to go meet them at the airport," Cat said. "I'll let you know what's happening, okay?"

"Okay," River said, trying to hold it together but having a really rough time.

As predicted, Parker was waiting for Kai when she arrived with Digger. Digger and Bandit made fast friends as Kai extended her hand.

"Are we finding her or recovering her body?" Parker asked.

"Don't know," Kai said, shaking her head.

Kai was dressed in BDUs, minus her insignia. Parker wore her navy blue BDUs with her PD badge on; she knew she was there in an official capacity. Catalina met them five minutes later, putting on her gear, including her vest, even as she got out of the car.

"You're going?" Kai asked.

"She's my responsibility," Cat said gravely.

Kai nodded, glancing at Parker, who winced slightly.

Skyler arrived in the Pave Hawk helicopter ten minutes later. The flight to San Diego didn't take too long, and en route she got a call from Shenin saying that the C-26 would be up and meeting them at Brown Field by the time they landed.

"I'm going to go up with the C-26," Cat said. "I'm putting you two down on the ground with the dogs. If we get a hit we can direct you. I've got units coming in from the PD, thanks to Kyle."

They'd just landed at Brown Field when Cat got a call. She walked away, talking on the phone. When she came back, she looked even more worried.

"They found her car. It's totaled, and it rolled at least three times. She wasn't in it, but there was plenty of blood."

"Fuck," Kai said, shaking her head. "Okay, get us to the crash site. We can use her blood to give the dogs the scent. We'll find her, Cat—if she's out there, we'll find her."

Cat nodded, her face like stone. She knew she needed to hold it together to try and find Sinclair—if nothing else, to give River a body to bury and closure. She held off on contacting River; she needed to see what they found first. Telling River about the wreck and Sinclair's blood would only freak her out.

One of the PD officers drove up and greeted Cat. She thanked him for coming and asked him to take Kai, Parker, and the dogs to the crash site.

Kai and Parker walked up to the Challenger, which lay on its roof. Rain was pouring down on them, but they didn't seem to notice. They gave the dogs the direction to the car and they both sniffed it thoroughly. They then gave the command to search. The dogs took off.

"This rain isn't going to help," Kai said.

"Nope," Parker said, shaking her head.

They headed off after the dogs.

It was two hours' and three miles' worth of walking before the dogs signaled something. They were on the edge of a deep ravine.

Parker called it in to Cat as Kai went to check out the ravine.

"Hold up!" Parker said. "Let's make sure we're alone out here. Bandit, pass auf!" she commanded, telling him to guard, as she pulled out her gun and held it up at the ready. "Okay, see what you can see," she told Kai, surveying the area.

Kai moved as far down the ravine as she could, shining a flashlight.

"I can't fucking see anything with this flashlight—we need a floodlight!" she yelled.

Parker got on the radio and relayed the request to Cat. Two minutes later a helicopter arrived and hovered, its floods turned on. Skyler's voice came over the radio.

"Just tell me where you need it."

"Sky, come right about five degrees," Kai said over the radio.

Parker crossed to the ravine as two police units arrived. She and Kai headed further down and started moving debris. Parker shifted a tree limb and uncovered a hand.

"Kai!" she yelled, kneeling to shift the dirt and rocks.

"It's her!" Kai shouted.

They quickly uncovered Sinclair. She was bleeding, but they couldn't tell from where. She was ice cold and unconscious.

Parker got on the radio. "Sky, get that copter down here. We're going to need to get her to a hospital the second we get her out of here. Get those guys down here!"

Ten minutes later they lifted Sinclair's still body out of the ravine. They got her to the helicopter and established that she did have a pulse, but it was faint. Her lips were blue and she was extremely pale.

Skyler headed for the nearest hospital, getting directions from local traffic control on the way. The last thing any of them wanted was to lose Sinclair now.

Chapter 9

River was frantic as they put her on the helicopter to take her down to San Diego. She'd been told that they'd found Sinclair and she was alive, but that was all. When the helicopter landed at Brown Field, Cat met River there with a car.

Cat drove at breakneck speeds as she explained to River what had happened.

"We found her car—it's totaled, and it looks like someone hit her going pretty damned fast, so they were trying to kill her. The car rolled a few times and ended up on its roof. Sinclair wasn't in it, but there was blood—the dogs were able to track her from that. We found her in a ravine half covered by mud and debris. We're damned lucky she didn't drown, which was probably what they expected to happen to her..." Cat trailed off as she looked over at River. She knew she was probably scaring the girl, but she needed her to understand how serious this was. "They've got her in the ER and they're working on her. I don't know a lot more than that right now; I wanted to be here when you got here."

"Okay," River said, sounding and looking terrified.

They got to the hospital twenty minutes later. Kai and Parker were in the waiting room, their dogs lying on towels the hospital had provided. It had been explained to the hospital staff that the dogs had been the ones to locate the missing officer. The staff had been more than happy to provide towels to dry off the dogs, as well as Kai and

Parker, who were thoroughly soaked.

"Do we know anything?" Cat asked.

Kai shook her head, reaching over to hug River, as did Parker.

"She's got a head wound, we know that for sure," Parker said. "There was a lot of blood, so I'm not sure where else she's injured."

Cat nodded, worried.

It was two hours before anyone came out to tell them anything. They would only speak to Cat, since she was Sinclair's boss and no "family" was present.

"Ms. Christensen suffered a severe head injury in the crash. She has a broken arm and a number of cuts and bruises, but the head wound is our biggest concern. At this point she's been unresponsive, and her scans show a lot of swelling. I'm afraid she's slipped into a coma. This may be a good thing, however, because it will allow her body to heal. But we're going to have to watch the head injury—it may be necessary to do a ventriculostomy."

Cat glanced at River, who nodded, understanding what the doctor was saying.

"Is she on oxygen?" River asked the doctor.

He glanced over at her, looking slightly surprised, but nodded. "We're also giving her fluids to try and counteract the swelling.

River nodded, trying to hold on to her emotions. This was Sinclair they were talking about, but she needed to understand what was happening.

"When can we see her?" Cat asked, knowing it was what River wanted to know.

"She's in recovery now—it'll be another couple of hours before you can see her."

Cat nodded, thinking they were already going to have an issue with getting River in there if this hospital was going to be a stickler about rules and "family" only. She walked over to Kai.

"See if Finley can get some time off and come down here," Cat said, leaning close. "I think we might need her professional assistance. I'll get her a ride down."

Kai nodded, pulling her phone out and making a call.

By the time they were allowed to see Sinclair, Finley, Rayden, Jericho, Gray, and Zoey had joined the group.

Finley had spoken to the doctor and explained who these people were—that they were essentially Sinclair's law enforcement family and the only ones able to travel down to San Diego at that point. She didn't mention Sinclair's wife, who was safely in Hong Kong.

River was the first to go in to see her. She was shocked by the way Sinclair looked; her eyes were darkened, bruised from the head injury. Her left arm was in a cast, and she had cuts on her face and hands. There was a bandage on her head. River reached over, touching Sinclair's cheek.

"You have to get better, babe," she said softly.

River stood listening to the machines beep and whir, doing her best not to think about what her life would be like without this woman in it. She'd fully embraced all the parts of Sinclair that she'd experienced. She'd forgiven everything and loved Sinclair more than anything. She hadn't even had a chance to introduce Sinclair to her family yet. Now she wished she had.

After a half hour or so, River came out of the room so the others could visit Sinclair. After everyone had seen her, Cat had River go back in.

"You're the one she's most likely to respond to, voice-wise," she said.

"You'd be surprised how well people in comas respond to loved ones," Finley added.

River nodded, willing to do whatever it would take to help Sinclair.

She spent the next six hours talking to her, until her voice was hoarse. She told her random things about her childhood, about getting her nursing degree, and on and on. She finally fell asleep, her head on the bed next to Sinclair's shoulder, her hand on Sinclair's.

It was the first thing Tracey saw when she marched imperiously into the room, followed by a doctor who was wringing his hands in concern. Tracey had already threatened to sue the hospital for carrying out procedures on Sinclair without authorization, and then for allowing people that weren't family members access to her.

"I want her out of here right now," Tracey said, pointing at River, who started awake.

"What?" River said as she looked over, her eyes widening when she saw Tracey.

"Fortunately the Department of Justice is wise enough to contact Clair's actual family when she disappears," Tracey sneered.

"She disappeared almost three days ago, Tracey," River said as she stood up.

"I had business to wrap up," Tracey said haughtily.

"Nice!" River said, wanting to smack the woman.

"Did you hear me?" Tracey snapped at the doctor. "I want her out!"

Finley, who'd come in behind Tracey and the doctor, walked over to River and put her arm around her shoulder.

"Come on," she whispered.

"That's right, get her out of here," Tracey said.

Finley narrowed her eyes at Tracey as she walked River out of the room.

"I'm sorry," she said to River. "I didn't want her to have them call security to remove you."

Out in the waiting room, Cat moved to hug River. "I had no idea they'd called her."

"They called her almost three days ago—she just now got here!"

"Yeah," Cat said. "She's a bitch, and we all hate her, but unfortunately she's still Sinclair's wife."

River nodded miserably. She knew Tracey wasn't going to talk to Sinclair as she'd been doing. It worried her.

Parker crawled into bed behind Talon. It was two days since she'd gone to find Sinclair.

Talon turned over immediately. "How's Sinclair?"

Parker had texted her from the hospital, giving her an update. "She's okay, but that bitch of a wife of hers isn't letting anyone see her," she said tiredly.

Talon wrapped her arms around Parker, pulling her close and kissing her lips. "You sound exhausted. Get some rest, babe."

"When do you leave?"

"Tomorrow at noon," Talon said, grimacing.

Part of the movie she was working on was being filmed in Morocco. The crew had already left, and the cast were going the next day. They'd be gone for three weeks to a month, depending on how filming went.

Parker snuggled closer to Talon, wanting to stay awake, but she hadn't slept more than a couple of uncomfortable hours in the last two days and her body wasn't cooperating. She was asleep a few moments later.

Talon held Parker against her, smiling sadly in the dark. She hated that she was leaving, and she was worried about the next day. She spent the next couple of hours thinking and rethinking her plan. In the end, she fell into a fitful sleep.

The next day, Parker drove Talon to the airport. As they got onto the freeway, Talon looked over at her.

"I want you to consider something for me while I'm gone…" she said, trailing off as Parker glanced at her.

"Okay…" Parker said.

"I want you to think about giving Chelle that second chance she asked you for."

Parker looked stunned by the statement, and then another expression took over.

"Why?" she asked simply.

"Because," Talon said, "you two have been together for twenty years, and you have a child together, and a grandchild. I just can't help thinking that I'm in the way of that."

Parker looked thoughtful, her lips set in a grim line. She nodded, but her eyes told Talon that she didn't believe what she was saying.

"What?" Talon asked.

Parker simply shook her head.

"You think I'm trying to get out of this, don't you?" Talon asked.

"I think you don't date people for long."

"You're right, I don't—but that's not what this is about, Parker."

"You sure about that?"

Talon reached across, touching Parker's hand. "Yes, I'm sure. I just need you to think about it, okay?"

Parker didn't look pleased with the request, and the rest of the drive was made in silence. At the airport, Talon slid over on the bench seat of the Cougar, wrapping her arms around Parker's neck, leaning in to kiss her. She could sense Parker's distance then, and was worried that she'd just caused irreparable damage to their relationship.

The fact was that if Parker belonged with Chelle, then that's who she'd be with—the last thing Talon wanted was to break up a family. Parker was right about her; she didn't stay with people for long. It was for that reason that she didn't want to mess up any chance that Parker would be happier back with Chelle.

As the plane left for Morocco, Talon looked out the window, hoping she hadn't just screwed up. Part of her didn't want to even think about Parker with Chelle, but she knew that she had done the right thing. It gave Parker the leeway to do what was in her heart to do, even if Talon felt like hers was breaking a little bit with the thought of it.

River was ready to chew nails. It had been two weeks, and she'd been coming to the hospital every day with the hopes that Tracey would finally give in and let people see Sinclair. Tracey hadn't budged an inch. She'd refused to let anyone in. River was in constant touch with the temporary nurse she'd gotten for Abe. Unfortunately, Abe had a cold and wasn't able to travel down to San Diego to see Sinclair. River was purposely letting him believe that everything was okay and Sinclair was recovering well. She couldn't take the chance that the news of her condition would upset him and cause his health to deteriorate. It was the least she could do for Sinclair at this point.

The doctors said Sinclair wasn't improving, and River was certain it had everything to do with Tracey being there. She was getting desperate, and at this point she didn't care—if she had to beat the shit out of Tracey to get to see Sinclair, she was doing it. Getting up from the chair where she'd sat off and on for the last two weeks, she marched down to Sinclair's room. Tracey was sitting across the room from where Sinclair lay, on her laptop. River walked straight over to Sinclair and sat down next to her.

Tracey's head snapped up. "What do you think you're doing in here?"

"I think I'm seeing the woman I love, and you can fucking call anyone you want, but they're going to have to drag me away from her."

With that, River reached over and took Sinclair's hand, searching her face. "Sin, I'm here, okay? I love you. Come back to me… please."

Tracey stood up and went over to the door, watching River as she did. River didn't even spare her a glance; she just kept staring down at Sinclair. Lowering her head, she put her lips next to her ear.

"I love you. Please come back to me… please…"

Tracey opened the door and stopped an orderly in the hallway, telling him to get a security officer.

River sat with her head against Sinclair's, ignoring Tracey.

"Just come back, honey… just come back…"

A security guard arrived and walked up to Tracey. "What's the problem?"

"I want this woman out of my wife's room," she said, pointing at River.

The guard stepped inside, looking over at River.

"She doesn't seem to be harming your wife," he said.

He'd seen River sitting in the waiting room for weeks now, and everyone in the hospital knew who she was. Tracey had treated every member of staff like they were beneath her, ordering everyone around. No one liked her.

"I want her the fuck out of here! Do your goddamned job!" Tracey screeched.

River turned to look over at Tracey, hoping she would give herself a heart attack with the stress of trying to control everything. That's when she felt Sinclair's hand squeeze hers. Snapping her head around, she looked down at Sinclair and saw the most beautiful blue eyes she'd ever seen staring back at her.

"Sin?" River said, praying she wasn't imagining it.

"Hi," Sinclair said softly.

"Hi…" River was so happy she could barely breathe.

Sinclair's eyes shifted to the security guard, who still stood looking at her. "You can get her out of here now," she said, nodding at Tracey.

River saw the security guard start to grin as he turned to Tracey. "I'm going to have to ask you to leave."

Tracey stared back at him, openmouthed. "Surely you're not serious?"

The guard's lips quirked in a grin. "I am serious, and don't call me Shirley."

River laughed, and Sinclair did too. Tracey, of course, didn't get it. The security guard ushered her and her laptop out of the room post-haste. There was a loud cheer down the hall moments later as everyone was informed that Sinclair had just awoken.

River turned to her, leaning down to kiss her softly on the lips.

"I heard you," Sinclair said.

"You did?"

"I heard you tell me to come back to you."

"I'm so glad you listened," River said as she stared down into Sinclair's eyes.

"How could I not?"

It took Parker three days before she realized Talon wasn't calling her. She knew it was Talon's way of "leaving her alone" so she could "give Chelle the chance she asked for." The words rolled around in her head so many times that Parker was ready to scream. Further, it was as if Chelle knew Talon's request was hanging out there, because she came to see the baby and Kim a lot more often suddenly, starting the day Talon left for Morocco.

On the fourth day that Talon had been gone, Parker was home with the baby; she had a bit of a cold and Kim had to work. She'd finally gotten Ginny to sleep when Chelle knocked on the door. She looked through the panes and could see Parker lying on the couch, the baby on her chest, so she opened the door quietly.

"Ruhig," Parker said to Bandit when he stood up, telling him to be quiet.

"You're home today?" Chelle asked. It was a Tuesday; normally Parker would be at work.

"Yeah, Gin's got a cold," Parker said. "Kim had to work."

Chelle nodded. "Well, I can stay with her if you need to go to work."

"I'm okay," Parker said, grinning. "It's kinda nice to have a day off in the middle of the week."

"Ah-ha! Using your granddaughter to shirk your responsibilities!" Chelle said, laughing.

"That's me."

"No, it's really not," Chelle said, shaking her head. "But it's really cute all the same." She moved to sit on the floor next to where Parker lay, looking at their granddaughter. "She really is cute, isn't she?"

Parker nodded.

"It's not just because we're her grandparents, is it?" Chelle asked.

"No, she's adorable," Parker said, canting her head to look down at Ginny fondly. "Thankfully she looks nothing like that asshole."

"She looks like Kim," Chelle said.

"She looks like you," Parker said, smiling.

Chelle smiled too.

"You scared the shit out of us," Cat said.

"I had no intention of scaring anyone," Sinclair said, sitting up in bed with River right next to her, holding her hand.

"So what happened?" Kai asked.

"It was Tony and Eddie," Sinclair said. "They were waiting for me. I just saw the flash of their faces—I never really saw the car they T-boned me with, but it sent me spinning." She grimaced. "Then it flipped. There was nothing I could do."

"Nope, just hold on and try not to die," Rayden said.

"Yeah," Sinclair said, holding up her broken arm. "This is what I got for that effort."

Rayden shook her head. "I saw your car—you're damned lucky to be alive."

"Especially after you ended up in that ravine we hauled you out of," Kai said.

"Yeah, I didn't end up there of my own accord, trust me," Sinclair said. "I really don't think they thought I was alive, but they weren't taking any chances. They probably hoped I'd wash out to the ocean."

River grimaced at the images Sinclair was creating.

"Sorry, babe," Sinclair said, squeezing her hand.

"Well, the good news is we'll get them for attempted murder of a peace officer," Cat said. "I've already got the Mexican police looking for them."

"Mexican police?" Sinclair asked. America almost never got help from Mexican police on cases against the cartel, and Tony was all cartel.

"Yeah," Cat said, grinning. "Midnight's friends with the police chief, has been for years now. He's doing her a favor."

"Whoa…" Sinclair said, looking duly impressed.

"Midnight's not real fond of officers of hers getting hurt," Cat said, winking at her.

"So how'd they make you?" Jericho asked. "Any idea?"

"Oh yeah," Sinclair said, glancing at River.

"It's because of me?" River asked, looking sickened by the idea.

"Babe, it means they would have used you against me, and they would have killed you."

"They almost killed you," River said.

"But they didn't. And you being safe is more important to me than anything. Okay?"

River shook her head. "I don't know if I'm ever going to understand the work that you guys do," she said, her eyes touching on Cat, Jericho, and Rayden before settling on Sinclair. "But I know for damned sure that you are the most incredible people I've ever met."

It was another two days before Sinclair was released from the hospital. Tracey hadn't attempted to return to her room, but Sinclair suspected she'd be waiting at the house in LA. Cat arranged for a flight

243

back on Joe Sinclair's plane, not wanting to put Sinclair through the hassle of a commercial flight, nor wanting to push her luck with the Air Force in getting another aircraft from them. Joe Sinclair was a personal and professional friend. At the Los Angeles airport, an Escalade arrived, driven by John Machiavelli, Joe's business partner, to take Sinclair and River home. Jovina was there to pick up Cat; everyone else had traveled back by then.

At the house, River helped Sinclair inside, and with John's assistance they took her into the master bedroom and got her onto the bed.

"Thank you," Sinclair said to John, reaching up to shake his hand.

"Anytime," John said, grinning.

After he'd left, River went down and checked on Abe, thanking the nurse that had been caring for him.

"Is my Sinclair finally home?" Abe asked.

"She is, but she's resting." River smiled. "I'm sure she'll come see you soon."

"At least my pretty nurse is back now," Abe said, winking.

"Flirt!" River said, laughing.

"You know it!"

"I'm glad you're feeling better."

"Maybe I'll come up and see her," Abe said, his blue eyes sparkling.

River went back up to the master bedroom and saw that Sinclair was sitting up, looking over at the wedding picture on the wall.

"Do me a favor—take that down and toss it, will ya?" Sinclair said.

River took the picture down, carried it out to the veranda, and left it outside.

"Any sign of her?" Sinclair asked.

"No," River said, but they both knew that didn't mean she was gone.

They found out an hour later that she was definitely not gone. They heard the front door open and close, and Tracey came strolling into the master bedroom. Sinclair was half sitting up, leaning against the pillows. River was sitting on the bed next to her.

"Why are you still here?" Sinclair asked Tracey tiredly.

"This is still my home," Tracey said mildly.

"I want you out of my house."

"We all want things," Tracey said, her eyes going to the space where the wedding picture had hung.

Sinclair grinned. "It's outside if you want it—otherwise I'm thinking about using it as kindling for a nice fire. Take it and get out of my house before I have you forcibly removed. Why don't you move into that nice place you've been keeping down in the city. You know, the one where that little Japanese girl you brought back from Tokyo on your last trip is living."

Tracey's eyes widened.

"I told you, I'm a cop—I know how to find evidence," Sinclair said, her grin outright evil, "and I believe embezzlement from my personal account is going to be considered an illegal act, so unless you want to end up in jail, I'd advise you to do exactly what I tell you

245

to. Move the fuck out of my house, give me the divorce I'm asking for with no strings, no alimony, no splitting shit, and give me back the 1.3 million that you stole… and maybe I'll let you stay out of jail and keep that job you're so fucking proud of."

Tracey stared at Sinclair, her expression shifting from shock to fear to simple resolve as she lowered her eyes and nodded. Without a word she walked out of the master bedroom.

River stared at Sinclair.

"When did you…" she said, shaking her head as her voice trailed off.

"I did some checking before I went back undercover. I got the last bits of info on my phone while I was in the hospital."

"Jesus, she stole from you?"

"She probably told herself it was community property, but she's wrong—it's not. I inherited that money before her and I got together, so it's mine, and if she doesn't give it back, I'll have her ass arrested," Sinclair said with a falsely sweet smile.

"Could you really get her fired?"

"It's because of my family that she has her job, and my family owns half of the studio she works for, so yeah, I could get her fired. I'm thinking she forgot about that part."

River pressed her lips together. "I guess she underestimated you."

"She always has."

River reached out to touch Sinclair's cheek. "I'm so glad to have you back now."

"I'm glad to be home," Sinclair said. "And I'm glad you're here with me."

"I'll be here with you for as long as you like."

"Can we just go ahead and make that forever then?"

River smiled. "I think I can make that happen."

"Good. Do that, will ya?" Sinclair said, leaning in to kiss her softly.

Tracey moved out of the house that day. Sinclair was kind enough to tell her she'd box up the rest of her "shit" and send it to her at the studio.

Later that day, Quinn texted to say that she was coming by to see her. Sinclair grinned. She'd known the celebrations would really start when everyone heard that Tracey was gone. When Quinn got to the house, however, she had River bring Sinclair out to the driveway.

Sinclair was stunned to see the green Challenger, completely restored.

"How the hell…" she said, looking around at the many members of the group who stood there.

"Parker, Lyric, Cody, Jet, and I did the work," Quinn said, grinning. "Devin and Harley used their exceptional computer skills to find and get the parts from all over the country. The richer half donated the cash to the endeavor, and Joe donated the use of his plane for us to go and get and/or pull the parts from other Challengers. She's completely authentic still."

Sinclair shook her head slowly, unable to fathom the amount of work that had needed to be done to make the Challenger drivable again. The body damage alone had been monumental.

"I don't even know how to begin to thank you all," she said, tears in her eyes.

"That's what friends do," Cat said.

"Not any of the friends I've ever had."

"Well, we're a whole new level," Quinn said, grinning.

"You can say that again," Sinclair said, nodding as she hugged each and every member of the group, thanking them over and over again.

A couple of days later, Parker walked into her bedroom. She wore her BDUs, and Skip, the brindle pit, as well as Bandit followed her. She'd started toward the bed to take off her boots when she glanced up and felt her heart jump. Talon sat on the bed, completely naked, looking at her expectantly.

"You just about gave me a heart attack," Parker said, her look pointed.

"Sorry," Talon said, her green eyes sparkling.

"I don't think you are," Parker said as she sat down and began unlacing her boots.

"No?" Talon asked, raising an eyebrow. "What if I show you that I'm sorry?"

Parker glanced back at her. "I don't know," she said. "I haven't heard from you in three and a half weeks—that's a lot to be sorry for."

Parker went back to unlacing her boots and kicked them off. She felt Talon at her back then, and immediately felt Talon's hands come around to start unbuttoning her shirt. In moments, Talon pulled the tails of the shirt out of Parker's BDU pants, exposing the dark blue DOJ T-shirt she wore underneath. Talon removed the shirt and pulled the T-shirt off as well. Her fingers trailed over Parker's exercise bra, caressing nipples that were already growing hard. She lowered her head to kiss Parker's neck. Parker's hands came up to cover Talon's hands as she turned her head, her lips finding Talon's immediately.

Talon reached up, undoing the bra and taking it off. Her hands slid over Parker's nipples, making her gasp against Talon's lips. She continued to touch her, exciting her beyond all reason.

"Tal…" Parker moaned against Talon's lips. "Babe… please…"

Talon moved her hands down to the BDU pants, unzipping them, then reached inside. Parker came against her hand immediately, her head against Talon's shoulder. Talon held her close.

Parker turned around to face Talon. Going down to one knee, she slid her hands over Talon's legs and pulled her closer to the edge of the bed, spreading her legs wider. Talon cried out as Parker's mouth descended on her, making her scream, both her hands in Parker's hair, holding her there. After Talon came twice, Parker picked her up and laid her back on the bed, moving over her, the material of the BDU pants rough against Talon's skin, only serving to excite her more. Talon came again quickly, wrapping her body around Parker's, pressing as close as she could possibly get.

Parker shifted off her long enough to take off the rest of her clothes, then came back to take her again, moving against her, stopping as Talon got excited and moving away enough to cause her to try and pull her back. After a minute, Parker would press over her again, exciting her again, only to stop and hold off. She teased her that way for half an hour, to the point where Talon was begging her.

"Don't ever abandon me like that again," Parker whispered

against Talon's ear, just as she slid her finger inside her, pressing it deeper with her body in a thrust, making Talon scream loudly in her release.

Afterward, Parker lay on her back, taking Talon with her, holding her close. Talon snuggled against her, breathing heavily.

"I missed you…" Talon said softly.

"All evidence to the contrary," Parker said dryly.

Talon didn't say anything for a long minute, her hand tracing patterns on Parker's shoulder.

"I was trying to give you space," she said.

"Space?" Parker repeated, grinning sarcastically. "That's the thing you kids say now to make your actions okay, right?"

"Parker—"

"Wait, let me get this straight," Parker said, holding up her hand to halt Talon's comment. "You wanted me to give Chelle a second chance—"

"I didn't *want* you to," Talon said. "I just didn't want to stand in your way of being happy with your family."

"I was happy with my family," Parker said. "And you."

"But—"

"No buts, Talon. I was happy with the way things were. Regardless, you asked me to give Chelle another chance, and yet, despite not knowing if I'd done that or not, you show up here and greet me naked," she said, her look pointed. "Explain."

Talon took a deep breath, blowing it out slowly. "I couldn't handle the thought of you being with her. I couldn't let you go as easily as I thought I could."

Parker nodded. "So you thought you'd show up here and get me to cheat on her if I was back together with her?"

Talon looked instantly ashamed, her eyes dropping from Parker's. "I didn't think of that," she said, then looked up at Parker. "Would you have done this if you two were back together? I mean… did you?"

Parker gazed back at her for a long moment, her look considering.

Talon waited, holding her breath, afraid that Parker was about to tell her that she and Chelle were back together and this had just been a goodbye.

"No," Parker said simply. "I'm not back together with my ex-wife."

"Ex-wife?"

"The divorce was final two weeks ago," Parker said. "If you'd have called me I would have told you."

"I know, but I was—"

"'Giving me space,' I know," Parker said. She put her finger on Talon's lips. "Tell you what, when I need your so-called 'space,' I'll let you know, okay?"

"So you didn't give Chelle a second chance?" Talon asked, her tone far too hopeful.

Parker narrowed her eyes at the girl. "I wouldn't say that…"

Chelle had accompanied Parker to the grocery store a week after Talon left for Morocco, saying she needed to pick up a few things. As they'd done for years, Parker pushed the cart with her list in hand and picked up items as she went, Chelle following along. Parker never deviated from her list; it had always been this way.

"Still using a list, huh?" Chelle asked, her tone slightly condescending.

"It's how I don't forget shit."

Chelle nodded, realizing the cuss word meant she'd just irritated Parker and backing off.

They continued along. In the aisle with the baby items Parker stopped and took a picture of the specific formula Kim was using for Ginny.

Chelle canted her head at her.

"Kim said she's having a hard time finding this particular kind," Parker said, sending the picture to Kim in a text with a note about where it was located.

"You know that's code for 'Buy it for me, Mom,' right?" Chelle said.

"Yep," Parker said. "And she's the one that wanted to have a baby, so..."

Chelle nodded, looking circumspect. Parker saw it.

"You think I should buy it for her?" she asked.

"I don't think it's bad to help her," Chelle said.

"She's living in the house rent-free—I think that's helping her."

Chelle pressed her lips together, not wanting to argue with Parker, but she'd never liked Parker's hard line on Kim needing to take care of herself. She knew it was a lot that Parker had convinced Kim to move home, and that Parker helped out with the baby; she just didn't see why she drew the line where she did.

To Parker, Kim needed to support herself and the baby. She didn't mind helping, but she refused to be completely used either. Kim was working and getting a decent wage, so she had the money to pay for things for the baby. Having Kim move home was what Parker had thought was best for both of them, but she wasn't going to start paying for the baby Kim had decided to have.

When they got back to the house, they put the groceries away and Parker grabbed a beer before walking out to the backyard and sitting down. Chelle joined her a minute later, and Parker looked over at her.

"You seem to be coming around more lately," she said. "Is there a reason for that?"

Chelle gave her a measured look. Finally she nodded. "Yes, I'm more comfortable when I know she's not going to be here."

"By 'she,' you mean Talon?"

Chelle nodded. "Yes."

"As far as I've ever seen, Talon's never said anything nasty to you, so why don't you want to be here when she is?"

Chelle was surprised by the question. "Because I don't like seeing you two together, that's why."

Parker pursed her lips. "You're jealous?"

"Duh, Parker," Chelle said, rolling her eyes. "You're dating a twenty-three-year-old movie star who obviously has you completely wrapped around her little finger. Why wouldn't I be jealous?"

"Completely wrapped around her little finger?" Parker sounded *amused.*

"You're saying she doesn't?"

"I'm saying you don't know Talon."

"I know she has you," Chelle said. "And she's not letting you go anytime soon."

Parker laughed at that, the sound hollow even in her own ears.

"Now that's where you're wrong," she said.

Chelle stared at Parker, surprised by her actions. "What are you talking about?"

"She's working at letting me go as we speak," Parker said morosely.

"How?"

"By pushing me at you. She said she wants me to think about giving you that second chance you asked for."

Chelle looked shocked. "Oh…" she said, her voice trailing off. Then her expression changed. "So have you thought about it?"

Parker nodded slowly, a far-away look in her eyes.

"And?" Chelle asked, holding her breath.

Parker looked thoughtful again for a long minute, then shook her head. "The thing is, Chelle, that nothing's really changed, except maybe you got bored with what's-her-name and now you're thinking I'm safe. The thing is, there had to be something wrong with our marriage if you could do what you did."

"I made a mistake, Parker."

"Yeah, you did," Parker said. "But I think it was just a symptom, not the problem, and the problem is that you weren't happy—maybe

you never were, I don't know."

"I was happy—we were happy."

Parker nodded. "I guess we were—at least, I always thought we were—but you weren't... In the end you weren't..."

"It was stupid, Parker—I was stupid. I was enticed by something new and shiny, and it was stupid."

Parker nodded again. "Yeah, it was stupid. You picked the wrong girl... but you see, I didn't."

"What?"

"You asked me before if I was in love with Talon, and the answer is yes, I am. Now whether or not that means jack shit to her, I don't know, but I do know that I'm not going backward here."

Talon stared back at Parker, her mouth open.

"Let's get something straight here," she said, still somewhat surprised. "I was not trying to let you go—I didn't want to let you go, Parker, I told you that. What I didn't tell you was that I love you."

"Okay," Parker said, looking surprised.

"You told her you're in love with me?" Talon asked.

Parker nodded.

"Why?"

"Because I am," Parker said, so offhandedly that Talon had to take a moment to assimilate it before she comprehended it.

"You're in love with me?" she clarified.

"Yeah," Parker said. "And I know exactly where that puts me."

"Where?"

Parker grinned. "Right between heaven and hell."

Epilogue

"If a woman isn't butch, then what is she?" Palani asked.

Kana glanced at her, perplexed. "Huh?"

"I mean, if you're a lesbian and you're not butch, then what would it be called?"

Kana looked at her for a long moment, grinning slightly. "I think you mean femme."

"Femme?"

"Yeah, the other side of butch."

Palani nodded. "So you'd be femme, right?"

Kana considered that, then shrugged as she went back to putting on her eyeliner. "I guess some might see it that way. I never really thought about it—I'm me."

Palani nodded. "So that's it then."

"What's what then?" Kana asked, lost again.

"Why you're not attracted to me at all."

Kana turned around, leaning against her sink. "Okay, tell me where your head just went," she said, her face indicating her confusion at Palani's logic.

"Well," Palani said, "femmes are interested in butch women, right?"

"Uh…"

"And I'm not even sort of butch, so that's why you're not attracted to me." Palani sounded proud of herself for figuring that out.

Kana laughed softly, shaking her head. "What makes you think that femmes are only interested in butch women?"

"Well, there's got to be one that plays the man and one that plays the woman, right?"

Kana laughed outright then. "Oh, baby girl, who told you that one?"

Palani stared back at her. Somewhere in her head she had caught the "baby girl" and liked it, but she didn't comment on it. "No one, really, I just…" she said, trailing off as she shrugged.

"Okay, well you're wrong," Kana said. "It's not about being femme or butch. It's not about whether you wear makeup, high heels, or nice clothes. It's about whether or not you have deeper feelings for women than you do men. There is no 'man' in the relationship—that's the whole point."

Palani bit her lip, trying to understand. "Have you always known you wanted women?"

"No," Kana said. "It took me a long time to figure it out."

Palani nodded. "So you dated men before that?"

"Yep, and none of them inspired any kind of deep love, or even deep feelings of attachment."

"But you feel that with women?"

"Yes," Kana said. "With women I feel like I can be myself and open up my heart. I'd never do that with a man."

Palani nodded, understanding what Kana meant. It was what she'd been struggling with. The problem was, she didn't know if it was just that she hadn't been with enough men to find the right one, or if she really did want to be with women.

"How do you know if it's just that you haven't met the right guy yet?" she asked, hoping someone could finally help her answer her own biggest question.

Kana looked back at her for a long moment. "Well, I'd say it's pretty simple, really," she said. "If you're only turned on by men, and not women, then you haven't met the right man yet."

"How would I know if I'm turned on by women if I can't ever find out?"

"Well, that's why you're looking for one, right?"

"Right."

"Well, there you go," Kana said, grinning.

She stood from the counter, turning to look in the mirror and putting the eyeliner away. She started to move toward the door.

Palani got up from the bed. "So, then, what is your type?" she asked.

Kana stopped in her tracks, glancing back at her. She grinned and shook her head.

"Never mind," she said, then proceeded out of the bedroom and back down the hall.

"Why?" Palani asked doggedly as she followed her.

Kana picked up her keys off the island, still grinning. "Just never mind." She started toward the front door.

"Kana!" Palani exclaimed, moving to intercept her, literally standing in front of the door so Kana couldn't open it.

Kana stared down at her, perplexed.

"What?" Palani asked.

"Who told you my name?" Kana asked.

"What is your type?" Palani countered.

Kana grinned again, shaking her head.

"Stop that!" Palani said, laughing softly.

"Who told you my name?" Kana asked again.

"What is your type?" Palani countered again.

Kana looked thoughtful for a moment. Placing a hand on the door above and behind Palani's head, she leaned down menacingly, her eyes glittering mischievously. "Tell me who told you."

"Tell me your type," Palani replied, putting her hands on her slim hips.

Without another word, Kana leaned in and kissed her lips softly. When Palani moaned quietly, Kana took a step forward, deepening the kiss.

Palani's hands touched Kana's waist, grasping at her as every nerve in her body seemed to come alive.

Kana pulled back, looking down into Palani's eyes.

"*You* are my type."

"I am?" Palani breathed, looking shocked.

"Smart, beautiful, petite, and very feminine," Kana listed. "Yes, you are my type."

Follow the author and find out more about her series here:

Website: www.sherrylhancock.com

Facebook: @SherrylDHancock

Twitter: @Sherryl_Hancock

Also by Sherryl D. Hancock:

The *MidKnight Blue* series. Dive into the world of Midnight Chevalier and as we follow her transformation from gang leader to cop from the very beginning.

www.vulpine-press.com/midknight-blue-series

The *Wild Irish Silence* series. Escape into the world of BJ Sparks and discover how he went from the small-town boy to the world-famous rock star.

www.vulpine-press.com/wild-irish-silence-series